ALISON BLAIR

Fanciful Tales by Gertrude Crownfield

JOSCELYN OF THE FORTS

PRINCESS WHITE FLAME

THE BLUE SWORDSMAN

THE FEAST OF NOEL

THE SHADOW WITCH

*Suddenly they were aroused by a
blood-curdling whoop*

ALISON BLAIR

by

GERTRUDE CROWNFIELD

Illustrated by
GEORGE M. RICHARDS

jC886z

Published by
The Blakiston Co., Philadelphia
Distributed by
E. P. Dutton & Co., Inc., New York

First printing . . . Mar., 1927
Second printing . Dec., 1927
Third printing . . June, 1928
Fourth Printing . . June, 1929
Fifth Printing . . July, 1931
Sixth Printing . Sept., 1935
Seventh Printing . Sept., 1938
Eighth Printing . . Dec., 1943

~~~~~~

To

DR. JOHN EASTMAN WILSON

this book is gratefully and respectfully

dedicated

Contents

List of Illustrations

The decorations for the title page and wrapper were also done by George M. Richards

ALISON BLAIR

Chapter i

IT was February in England in the year 1755. Perched on a southern wall in a garden in Kent, a girl drooped her brown locks over an apricot bough, and pried back the scales from one of its tightly folded buds.

"Oh, Roger!" she called down, "they are still quite sound asleep, and Spring nearly two months away. I would 'twere not so, for I pine to smell the sweet things."

The old gardener, digging in the soft loam of the garden beds that lay along the ruddy brick wall, rested on his spade.

"Sweet enough, sweet enough, Miss Alison," he agreed, rubbing his horny hands upon his coarse linen smock, "and there'll be as fine a crop of fruit this year as ever she bore. A tidy little tree, she be, be she blooming or fruiting. She earns her winter's rest."

"A tidy little tree," laughed Alison Blair, speaking to the dormant tree. "Roger calls you tidy. 'Tis his best word of praise. But when you bloom, I call you lovely sweet—enchanting lovely."

"Tidy be a good word, Miss Alison. It says a mort o' things for me," maintained the old man stoutly, going back to his task of bringing up great spadefuls of earth, and giving to each a sounding thwack when he had turned it over.

"Surely it does, Roger," teased the maid. " 'Tis a tidy tree, a tidy little nag, a tidy pat of butter, a tidy lad."

"Ay," returned Roger, with an upward glance at her face, set like a rose among the naked boughs, "and a tidy lass, too, mayhap. Tidy every one o' them in his own way."

"And the crocuses—the darlings! We must not forget those, Roger, for you know you think them the tidiest of all."

Roger nodded assent. His crocus borders were the finest in the county, as he well knew. He stuck his spade upright in the rich mold, and left it there while he crossed the lawn to see whether, by good chance, some delicate purple or golden head might already be piercing the moist, dark soil.

Swinging her feet idly in the sunshine, Alison let her red camlet cloak slip from her shoulders, and began to sing an ancient ballad, softly at first, but presently in fuller voice:

> "Springe is ycommen in,
>   Dappled lark singe;
>   Snow melteth,
>   Runnell pelteth,
>   Smelleth wind of new buddinge."

The words floated clear and sweet to the ears of her father, just entering his garden gate. A fine tall figure of a man was Dr. Matthew Blair. Although still in the prime of life as he was, his thick chestnut hair was beginning to show a trace of silver. It was bound into a neat queue, and with cocked brown beaver atop, it covered a head filled with more than the common share of knowledge, and of wisdom. Beneath his snowy linen ruffles, and the fawn-colored satin vest that set off his handsome broadcloth coat of russet brown, beat as warm and kind a heart as was ever given to human being. His feet, trimly shod in low-cut, silver-buckled shoes, and long silken hose, went on countless errands of mercy and relief of pain. Now, with a brightening of his deep gray eyes, and a smile that rose as a light on his grave face, he quickened his steps to reach the daughter who was the very apple of his eye.

"A blithe spirit, she has—my little lass," he thought. "May naught cloud it!"

From her perch upon the wall, Alison spied him coming, and in a moment was upon the ground, and running to meet him.

"For once you are at home in time for tea!" she exclaimed, as she answered his kiss of greeting. " 'Tis well-nigh a miracle!"

"Miracle indeed," quoth he, laughing down at her, "with Philip Meadowes just back from London town, where he has walked at Saint Bart's Hospital a full year, and with all that he has to say of that, and of other matters. But let's to our tea, and there I'll tell you of what he's been pouring into my ears this hour back."

Along the graveled path to the quaint old Tudor cottage they went together, she clinging to his arm as her tripping feet strove to keep up with his longer, steadier pace, and together they went through the broad low door, wreathed with ivy, and passed into a dim hall, where Alison cast down her cloak upon an oaken chest, and Dr. Blair discarded his broad beaver.

"Oh, 'tis a grand gay fire that Martha has

lit for us," cried Alison, "and see, she has the table set betimes."

She had gone before her father into the drawing-room, where the cheerful blaze flung brightness to the oak-beamed ceiling overhead, danced in flickering gayety along the time-darkened polished wainscot, made more mellow the ivory keys of the ancient spinnet, and repeated itself in every glassy surface of the colored prints upon the walls, and in the tiny leaded panes of the mullioned windows.

"And here is our tea," added Dr. Blair, sinking into his favorite chintz-covered armchair with a sigh of content, for through an opening door at the farther end of the room came Martha, bringing the welcome tray.

If Alison, in her crimson damask gown, and daintily ruffled kerchief, was the sweet flower of youth, old Martha was the frost-wrinkled fruit of kindly age. Very like to a withered apple was her face under its starched mob cap, and she moved a bit stiffly in her stiff dress and rustling apron whilst she set down the tray, and arranged the porcelain cups, and plates of thin bread and butter, and delicately browned tea-cakes.

"See, father, Martha has made your favorite cakes," burst forth Alison.

"Aye," nodded Martha, her ruddy face aglow. "Master be fond o' them, but so be little mistress, too."

Alison, taking her cup from the old woman's hand, dimpled at her sally. "And little mistress, too," she echoed roguishly, as she reached out for the delicacy.

She settled herself upon a tapestried footstool by her father's side, and began at once to sip, and to nibble, and Martha, having served them both, rustled away to the sunny kitchen to give her good husband, Roger, his afternoon cup.

Dr. Blair, taking his tea leisurely, let his eyes rove from his child's soft grace to this or that pleasant spot in the ordered peace of the ancient room, but always brought them back to rest thoughtfully upon her again.

Alison emptied her cup, and set it down.

"Now, father," she demanded coaxingly, resting her elbows upon his chair-arm, and looking up at him with her chin set on her folded hands, "what are these tales that Philip Meadowes has been pouring into your ears this afternoon? I have been monstrous patient whilst you took your tea, but you must not try me overmuch."

"Methinks it was none too sore a trial while you were taken up with your cakes," laughed

Dr. Blair, "but now you shall hear. Being a maid, you will care less to know what he told me of the multitude of beds in St. Bart's, and the sick folk who languished in them, and the nature of the draughts dealt out to them for their betterment, than you will be to learn that he has betrothed himself to one, Mistress Lettice Howard of London town, who, so he tells me, is of a quite ravishing loveliness and charm."

"Philip Meadowes betrothed!" exclaimed Alison, her eyes wide with surprise. "That is news, indeed! And doth he marry soon?"

"It was of that that he most wished to speak with me," returned the Doctor, stretching his weary feet nearer to the hearth, for its warmth was grateful, as the chill of the February twilight crept down. "At first Philip had been all for going overseas to our colonies in the Americas, there to take up the practice of his art, for he hath a taste for adventure, and would try his fortunes in the New World."

"And this he may, being a man," sighed Alison enviously. "'Tis women and old folk and maids who must bide close at home, and see naught of the curious sights in foreign parts."

"Mistress Lettice is not of your mind, lass," replied her father. "She will hear naught of it, and gives him to understand that if he would wed with her, he must stay in her own England."

Alison tossed her shapely head in disapproval. "Were I Philip Meadowes," she declared flatly, "I should betake myself to the colonies if it seemed good to me, and Mistress Lettice might follow me, or stay behind, as she listed."

Dr. Blair regarded his downright little lass with amused eyes. "You know naught of love, Alison," he commented, "nor how it molds the plans of man and maid. But so far as Philip is concerned, he is well content now to tarry in England if so be he can find what suits his needs and his lady love's desires in an abiding-place."

"This much I know," quoth Alison, "for love of you, I would follow you to the world's end, and so might Mistress Lettice follow Philip Meadowes had she love enough for him." She dropped her head to her father's knee, and gazed into the red embers from thence. " 'Tis a sad waste of a fine chance," she contested presently. "For myself I should vastly like to see our colonies, with their strange new life."

Dr. Blair opened his lips to reply, but left his words unsaid.

"Nor is't so savage there, neither, as Mistress

Lettice mayhap thinks," went on Alison dreamily, "for when I talked last sennight with Sir John Grayson's nephew, he told me that in New York they had the fashions, that gentlemen went in wigs and satin coats as they do here, and that the ladies were prodigious gay in their dress. He said that great cargoes of silks, and velvets, and 'broideries, and every sort of conceit, and handsome furnishings beside, were carried there from the Indies, and other foreign parts. Moreover, he did sit down to a grand banquet in as fine a house, he said—it was Governor Delancey's if I mistake not—as any in our own England."

"His tale was of the city of New York, little lass, though he might have said the like of Albany, or Philadelphia, or Boston town, but settlements are for the most part small, and distant one from the other, and savagery and rude ways of living are not far to seek."

"One needs not to seek them," asserted she. "Ralph Grayson saw naught of either, but did spend much time, instead, among the tulip and rose gardens, and flower beds, that stretch from the quaint Dutch houses to the broad East River. Indeed, he did even see a company of players in 'King Richard Third' whilst he sojourned in New York, though he did confess them shocking bad in their several parts."

"So if my dear lass were Mistress Lettice she would go?" inquired the Doctor, bringing his gaze from the red coals to rest it searchingly upon the girl's face.

" 'Tis like enough that I would go, being Alison Blair, had I sufficient reason thereto," spake she without hesitation.

Dr. Blair leant to his daughter, and drew her closer. "Shall we go, then, you and I?" he asked.

At the unexpectedness of his question Alison drew back in surprise. "What mean you, father?" she breathed. "You cannot be in sober earnest." Her gray eyes, wide and eager, sought his own in interrogation. But he met her eyes quietly.

"It is this," he explained, speaking slowly, and almost with hesitation. "More than once I have been fain to see our colonies for myself. In your sweet mother's lifetime I could not have thought of going without her, nor of asking her to leave, even for a day, the home that she loved so dearly. But now she is gone, and Philip Meadowes would rejoice at the chance of practicing in my stead for a year whilst I went abroad. For him it would be so much of experience, and for me so much of refreshment. However, it rests with you, my daughter, for if I go thither, I should take you with me, but I go not at all if you should give an unwilling consent."

Alison was swift with her answer. "I am no Mistress Lettice Howard," she cried, her eyes a-sparkle. "I go, and go gladly. Yet one thing you must promise me," she added, growing grave on a sudden. " 'Tis that you will not adventure yourself among the savages."

"Ay, that I can promise, my precious lass," declared the Doctor freely, "for it is but to New York, to Boston, and mayhap to Philadelphia that we shall go, and to such near-by spots beside as may be safe for you."

"And we shall return when the year is done," asserted Alison, springing up gaily. "What tales I shall have then to exchange with John Grayson!"

Away she went to cry the news to Roger and to Martha, and those good souls began straightway to bewail it loudly. The perils of wide sea, and frail, tossing ships, the dangers of wild shores, and wilder savages, loomed tremendous in their fancy, and they saw the Doctor and his child, to whom they were devotedly attached, and whom they had long served, torn from them, never to return. Naught that Alison could relate of tulip or crocus borders by Hudson or East River shores, or along the Bouwerie, of rustling silks or powdered wigs along Wall Street, could convince these two, against their previous conceptions, of what the colonies contained.

"Nay, nay, my pretty," protested Martha, her lip a-tremble, "'tis no safe place for a tender lass to go, for they do say that painted heathen roam there, and that the very hair hath been scalped from the heads of innocent women and babes," and groaning aloud in her distress, she pushed her snow-white mobcap wofully awry.

Roger, for his part, could but throw up his hands to heaven, and shake his head in speechless dismay, and naught that Alison, nor the Doctor himself, could say was sufficient to calm their forebodings.

Nevertheless, the decision had been made, preparations for the voyage began to go forward, and passage was engaged upon the sturdy ship *Neptune*, sailing in March for the distant port of New York.

Chapter ii

FROM a sheltered nook on the *Neptune's* deck Alison looked out over a sea stretching its unbroken waters to the horizon's rim. The sun, a fiery disc, fast setting, cast its last rays upon the crest of every tossing wave, and, caught there, the ruddy splendor was borne on and on, until the whole vast moving surface bore the semblance of a seething cauldron of molten copper.

But though the eyes of Alison were turned toward the glory in the west, her thoughts traveled eastward to her home in England, that she had left well-nigh three weeks ago. Dear and familiar were the woods and fields of Kent, peaceful, and safe, and happy. The pleasant house where she was born, shaded by ancient oaks and elms, sun-flecked, and set about with vines and garden closes—how near it still seemed! It was almost as though she could stretch out her hand, and touch its walls. Had she not felt sure that in a year, at most, she and her father would return to it, homesickness would have overwhelmed her.

Faithful Martha, who had watched over her from her infancy, had wept in bidding her "dear lamb" farewell, and Roger could scarce trust himself to speak. Alison had not been without her own tears, but these had been quickly dried by the adventurous spirit of youth, and her eagerness to behold new scenes.

What tales she had heard of this land toward which she was journeying: tales of rude pioneer life, of Indian massacre, of struggles by zealous priests and hardy soldiery to gain possession of vast tracts of territory in the name of church and monarch; yet running like a bright thread through all the dark warp and woof of these tales was the account John Grayson had given her of the life of the people in New York and Albany, and, since it was to the towns that she and her father were going, with the wild life they would have naught to do.

The ship ploughed on through the shining flood. From a mast overhead a Portuguese sailor lowered himself, and with something of a cat's stealth, and lithe agility of movement, came to deck. His dark bulk crossing Alison's vision as he passed her on his way below called back her thoughts from her far distant home, and directed them to himself.

Black José, his shipmates called him. Short, wiry of build, swarthy of skin, and rugged of feature, a great scar upon his left cheek, his small black eyes had a restless furtive shift under the gloom of his shaggy brows and rough black hair. Surly, and brief of speech, he was as dark of mood as he was of aspect.

Alison following him with her eyes, wondered at the glowering, defiant look upon his face, when there seemed naught to call it forth. A kindly captain, a crew who were genial and comradely enough among themselves, and cheerful about their duties, made this one sullen figure, who shunned all intercourse with his fellows, the more conspicuous by contrast.

When Dr. Blair ascended, directly afterward, the same companionway which had swallowed up the Portuguese, he found her pondering.

"Uncommon grave you seem for my cheery Alison," he commented, touching her cheek. "What may be the occasion?"

"Black José, father," replied she, rising to lean with him upon the ship's rail. "So sour of look he is, from morn till night. Not once, in all these days of our voyaging, have I seen smile on his face, or heard chanty from his throat. Why is he so different from the rest, I wonder."

"A melancholy soul, indeed, with something of wildness in his eye," returned Dr. Blair. "Mayhap his mind is a bit touched by some trouble, or grief, though doubtless he is harmless enough, poor man, for all his surly ways."

"Oh, think you he is crazed?" cried Allison, all soft pity. "Poor man, in truth!"

"Nay, not so bad as that," said Dr. Blair. "Perhaps no more than a melancholy. But come, my little lass, dwell no more upon it. Tell me, instead, how you have spent this last hour."

"Roving the seas," smiled Alison. "Backward to England, forward to the new shores. Behind us are so many friends. It will seem most strange to come to a land where we have none, nor any kith or kin."

"We cannot say, lass, that we shall be quite without kin, for in the Mohawk, your mother's cousin, one Captain Walter Butler, has his mansion. But the Mohawk country lies distant from New York, and west from Albany, and I think not to adventure so far inland. Moreover, we have no acquaintance with one another, nor did Captain Butler ever see your mother more than once, perhaps, for he, who is now an aged man, left England while she was still in her early childhood."

"I would fain see him, since he is our kinsman," spoke Alison, "but I should fear to go among savages to find him."

"The way is safe enough, if I may trust what Captain Knox has told me," answered Dr. Blair. "From New York to Albany sloops travel weekly, carrying goods and passengers on the great stream called the Hudson, and westward from Albany a broad highroad, set with farmhouses and prosperous farms, runs to Captain Butler's mansion, and far beyond it. But 'twould be a long hard journey for my little maid, so we'll not think on it."

From that the talk passed to other matters, until the summons came to supper in the cabin.

The evenings on shipboard were brimming with pleasures for Alison. The meal, served in sailor fashion, was so seasoned by the Captain's jests that the uncertain voyaging of food and drink from plate and cup to mouth, because of the heavy rolling of the sea, became cause for merriment and laughter. After the table was cleared, and the ship's lantern burned brightly where it swung from the low ceiling of the cabin, she gave charmed attention to the long

sea-yarns of Captain Knox, told to her father
and herself between strong puffs at the stubby
pipe held firmly in a corner of the old seaman's
mouth.

Tonight, before he was fairly launched, Alison asked him of Black José, and how it chanced
that he was the only foreign sailor among a
ship's crew of British.

"I've no fancy for Spanish or Portuguese,"
confessed the Captain, frankly. "A gloomy lot
they are. But we pick up crews as we can. I
was short an able seaman the day before we
sailed, and José stood by the waterside idle; so
I took him. He tends his duty with the best, but
he's no pleasant shipmate for the rest of 'em,
for there's days when he never opens his mouth,
and days when he mutters and scowls over his
work as if he had Old Horny himself for company."

From this Captain Knox plunged straightway
into a stirring tale of the Spanish Main, with
hair-breadth escapes from bearded pirates and
buccaneers, and Alison, listening with bated
breath, felt as though the cabin veritably
swarmed with a score or more of José's like,
heads bound about with scarlet silk, wide sashes
flowing, glittering cutlasses sweeping men down

ruthlessly. Even when she had said good-night, and gone to her berth, while her father tarried for a game of chess with the Captain, the gripping tale still filled her brain.

In spite of that, however, she fell fast asleep to the steady rolling of the ship, and knew no more until an insistent knocking upon her door aroused her.

"Miss Alison," called a voice, and again, and louder, "Miss Alison!"

She recognized the voice of the Captain, and something in its tone filled her with vague alarm.

"Yes, yes," she answered, springing from her berth. "What may you want, Captain Knox?"

"Your father needs you. You'd best come quick."

Alison's heart leapt to her throat. What was it that made him need her in the dead of night, and why could he not have come to her?

Asking herself this anxiously, she threw on wadded robe over her nightdress, thrust bare feet into slippers, and undid the door.

"What is't with my father?" she demanded, confronting Captain Knox. His "laddie-lass" her father had oft-times called her, for Alison, maid though she was, had something of lad's courage when occasion was. She had need of it now, and she summoned it, steadying her trembling lips, stilling her trembling, to meet this emergency, whatever it might be.

The Captain took her hand, and drew her away to her father's cabin, speaking to her low and hurriedly meanwhile. "It was Black José," he told her. "On a sudden he went mad, and hid himself, with knife in hand, to spring out on the first who passed him, no doubt. Your father, going to his berth——"

Alison interrupted him, crying beneath her breath, "He struck my father?"

"Ay," was the reluctant answer.

"And is he sore wounded?"

"Sore, sore, my poor lass. But bear ye up, child, he's not yet gone."

"Not yet gone." The words were as a cold hand clutching at the heart of Alison, but by a violent effort she stilled her trembling, for they were at her father's door.

"Bear up, lass, bear up," counseled the Captain, fearing lest she might give way.

"Have no fear for me," she replied, and laid her hand upon the latch.

Raised high in bed, that he might the better get his breath, lay Matthew Blair, white to the very lips. He, who had always smiled to greet his daughter, essayed to do so now, but could not for very agony. Black José's knife had struck home.

"Alison," he gasped, as she entered, "quick—in the chest—the small green vial."

She sprang instantly to obey, raised the lid of his brass-bound chest, found and opened the box of medicines, seized the precious vial with lightning fingers, and was at his side.

"Ten drops," prayed Matthew Blair.

She measured them with unfaltering hand, gave them, and presently saw the faint color stealing slowly to his face and lips.

"My parchment-covered packet—pen—and paper."

The words came with less strain, yet heavily.

She found these, too, and brought them.

"Write," he bade her.

Alison dipped the pen, and wrote as he gave the words.

To Captain Walter Butler, in the Mohawk country:

For the sake of your kinswoman, Alison Doane, guard her child, Alison Blair, and send her back to Kent, in England, under safe convoy. I, Matthew Blair, her father, dying at sea, send her to you with this packet, and this urgent prayer.

This he uttered haltingly, pausing only so much as was needful to rally failing breath and strength.

"Dying"—that one word blurred all the rest for Alison in a thick mist of tears that she tried in vain to hold back. Yet she wrote obediently and steadily to the final word. Then she threw down the pen.

"No, father—dearest. Not dying," she protested, in anguish. "It cannot be. You would not leave your Alison."

"Ah, my poor laddie-lass," he moaned faintly, " 'tis cruel—as a thousand deaths—to leave you, yet—I must."

Under the wavering light of the lantern, she saw him turn more ashen gray—saw the tide of color recede from his lips leaving them paler than before.

With forlorn hope, she snatched again at the medicine, thinking to revive him as she had before, but he made a sign to stay her.

Trusting, even in that supreme moment, in his superior wisdom, she obeyed him mutely, and set down the vial.

" 'Twould not avail me now," he whispered, with stiffening lips. His eyes sought Captain Knox, and his voice, scarce audible, adjured him solemnly: "You will send my daughter to her friends."

"Ay, ay, sir," promised the Captain, drawing nearer, to lose no word that the dying man might say to him.

"To Captain Butler in the Mohawk," murmured Matthew Blair anxiously.

"Ay, ay, sir," repeated Captain Knox, bending over him. "I'll do so; never fear."

Matthew Blair groped for his daughter's hand, that met and held his in the clasp of despairing love. His eyes, glazed by the mists of death, spoke her a last message of yearning tenderness.

Alison, knowing that it was farewell, bent to kiss him, and doing so, something of her mother's spirit rose in her, seeking to comfort him.

"Do not be afraid for me, dearest—there is God," she faltered.

"Ah, yes—there is God," he answered, "to Him—I leave you." And, with one long-drawn sigh of resignation, he was gone.

Chapter iii

A STRANGE hush fell upon Alison. She
sank upon her knees beside the low berth,
clinging to her father's icy hand, the hand that
heretofore had ever been warm and quick to re-
spond to hers, but could do so no more. In
her heart was a numbing grief, and her brain was
stunned with the shock of her tremendous loss.

Little more than an hour ago, Matthew Blair
had sat in the full tide of health and strength by
the table in the cabin, had laughed at the Captain's jests, and a little earlier still had bid her a
tender good-night before she went to rest. He
had spoken compassionately of the morose and
sullen creature who had robbed him of his life,
a life which held in it such rich possibilities of
continuing usefulness to his fellow beings, a life
so infinitely precious to her.

Her dark head resting on that breast which
had been her shelter, her happy refuge since first
she drew breath, felt it as rigid and cold as his
hand. He who had never seemed absent from
her in spirit before, now seemed removed to an

immeasurable distance. It was the sense of this that, flooding in upon her as she knelt, brought in its train a swift rush of scalding tears—merciful vent to her pent-up grief. Shaken with sobs, murmuring disconnected words of love and lamentation, she wept unrestrainedly, and Captain Knox, standing near in quiet sympathy, let the tide of woe sweep over her, for a while, unchecked.

But at last he stooped, and putting a brawny arm about her, drew her, half-resisting, to her feet.

"Come, come, my lass," he counseled her, his voice gruff with feeling, "give over crying for a little. True enough, your father's gone, and a rare fine man he was, but happen he's not gone so far as you think. Happen you'll feel him close by, many a time, if you're a good lass, always, and a brave one."

"A good lass, and a brave one." Borne down with sorrow as Alison was, the words pierced to her consciousness, came to her as a call from her father's very self, for many a time, as child and growing girl, she had been bidden by him to be both good and brave. Moreover, had she not told him, in his passing, that God would guard her? The thought of it had brought comfort to

him in that last moment, and it yielded to her a ray of that same comfort now. By a valiant effort she dried her tears, and raised her drooping head.

"You must get to your berth, Miss Alison," said the Captain, with kindly authority. "You're fair worn out."

"Oh, let me stay and watch by father," she pleaded, with beseeching eyes, "I cannot bear to leave him."

"No, no," refused Captain Knox, "you'll come away at once with me. When I've seen you to your door, I'll come back here myself, and watch him. And remember, Miss Alison—your father had my promise, and you shall be sent safely to your kinsman in the Mohawk when we reach port."

Bereft of her father's protecting care, the lonely child was seized with an intense homesick longing for England, and the kind old servants that she knew. This strange cousin, Captain Walter Butler, whom she had never seen, might or might not be kind. "I would that I need not go to the Mohawk," she protested, with quivering lip. "I would that I might go home at once to Kent."

"And so you might, Miss Alison," the Captain answered, "if so be I were sailing straight back to London from New York; but 'twill be the better part of a year before the *Neptune's* homeward bound. We touch at the West Indies, and many another port on our way for cargoes, and that your good father knew. Captain Butler will find you safe conduct, and you'll reach home a deal sooner than if I took you with me on the *Neptune.*"

Stretched out upon her berth in the darkness, Alison lived over in memory all that had happened since that hour on deck when José's scowling face had come between her and the glowing sunset sky. When at last she sank into troubled sleep, it was she whom the Portuguese pursued and threatened with uplifted knife, and always her father came between, and received in his own heart the blow directed at hers.

From this dream she would awake shuddering, only to dream again, and the dream and the awakening were always the same.

With the first dawn she arose, wan and heavy-eyed, and dressing hastily, crept away to her father. There, looking down upon his silent face, she beheld a calm so profound and majestic, a peace so deep, that the horrors of the night could not stand before them, nor in a presence thus angelic could she give way to noisy grief, or insistent yearning. It was rather as though a part of that celestial sphere that encompassed him stole out to her, soothing her aching heart, and loneliness of spirit.

From that moment, except in the brief periods when, yielding to the Captain's insistence, she tried to eat, or force herself to sleep, she sat beside her father, in part that she might feel that quieting influence, even though her tears often fell silently and fast, in part because she knew that the time was close at hand when she should look upon his beloved face no more.

That time arrived, and she heard the brief burial service read over him by Captain Knox, whose voice, grave and compassionate, lacked something of its usual steadiness as he uttered the solemn words. He would have drawn her away when the moment came for lowering the shrouded form into the deep, but Alison would not have it so, and remained standing at the ship's rail, her eyes, through their heavy mist of tears, straining after that form until the restless waves closed over it, and it was gone.

In the days that followed her trust in God and her courage stood her in good stead, and she took her sorrow quietly for one so young.

Black José had been put in ward until they should reach land, and while he clanked his chain, and clashed his manacled hands together, he rolled his reddened eyes, and betrayed by his ravings and his threats the fixed delusion that, long hidden, had urged him at last to furious act. It was that some day, when the waters of the sea should turn to molten copper, he would meet an Englishman, whom he must kill, unless he would himself be killed. Descending from the rigging on that fateful evening when he had seen the coppery glow of sunset upon the waves, the conviction had leapt into his brooding mind that the time was close at hand. He needed only to meet the Englishman, Matthew Blair, upon the companionway, to be sure that the man whom he must kill was before him, and so he had lain in wait for him when night had fallen, and struck when opportunity offered.

While Alison tried to bear her sorrow with fortitude, and Black José raged, the *Neptune*, favored by wind and tide, drew rapidly near to port. Low shores were dimly seen in the distance, wild land birds were descried, flying out across the tossing waters, and at last a pilot-boat came out to meet the vessel, and convoy it safely into the harbor of New York.

With what different feelings Alison awaited the landing from those which she had anticipated would be hers, when, with a blithesome heart, she had left England with her father to go upon a year of pleasuring. The skies overhead were as bright and blue as she had guessed they might be, the shores as freshly green as she had ever hoped to find them, but the face of all her little world was changed, and over her future hung a veil that her youthful vision had no power to pierce.

Carried securely in her bosom was the packet, and the letter, that her father had given her, and upon these rested her power to prove herself kin to that stranger in the unknown Mohawk country, Captain Walter Butler, bloodcousin to her mother.

Captain Knox had done his utmost to cheer the desolate girl, the sailors, touched by her orphaned state, had been kind in their rough, untutored fashion, so that she had not felt herself friendless on board the ship; but with the time so close at hand when she should be consigned to a guardianship totally strange, on shores as strange, it was no cause for wonder that beneath her quiet bearing her spirit quailed.

The ship, with the pilot on her bridge, passed

Sandy Hook, sailed steadily through the quieter waters of the Lower Bay, and on through the Narrows into the Upper Bay. In her course she left behind her many a pleasant stretch of green and richly cultivated farmland set with ample farmhouses, nestled among protecting trees. Huge barns stood in sunny open spaces. Farmland and orchard alike were touched by the first, delicately bright, verdure of Spring.

At last the city itself was seen, a host of sailing craft, of every size, and sort, and kind, anchored at its docks. Handsome houses, surrounded by wide grounds and gardens, stood upon the river banks, and from countless opening blossoms floated rich gusts of perfume mingling deliciously with the salt breeze from the Bay.

Wrapped in her heavy cloak, Alison, on deck, looked out upon the slow-moving panorama. At her feet was her portmantle. Her small traveling chest, and her father's also, securely corded, had been carried below, ready for landing.

The ship drew in. Captain Knox took his place upon the bridge to dock his ship, and in a moment more her anchor was dropped at Murray's Wharf.

With the lowering of the gang-plank, a crowd

of people who had been waiting on the dock for the coming of the *Neptune*, swarmed across it, and on to the ship. All manner of business had brought them thither. Custom-house officers first, to inspect the incoming cargo; then factors, eager to learn whether orders, sent to England in behalf of their customers on the vessel's last crossing, had been filled. Householders were there to purchase farm and family servants from among the redemptioners who had crossed in the hold. Others sought eagerly expected letters or parcels from relatives and friends in the mother country. Petty tradesmen clamored their wares. Gangs of porters and negro slaves prepared to fetch and carry. Bales, boxes, hogsheads of merchandise began to roll across the wharf in barrows and hand trucks toward the enormous warehouses near by.

Shrinking apart from all this bustle and confusion, awaiting the moment when she must leave the *Neptune*, Alison dreaded more and more bidding farewell to Captain Knox, whose sturdy presence had been as a bulwark to her in these last, sad, slow-moving days. A wild impulse seized her to rush away into the deepest darkest corner of the hold, there to conceal herself until the *Neptune* was again under way, to be carried back to England when and how the vessel might bear her thither.

But had she gone so far as to yield to this impulse she would have been checked at the outset, for even as it surged up within her, she heard the brisk step of the approaching Captain, and with him came a landsman's footfall, heavy, and unfamiliar. US M785810

Alison turned apprehensively. Behind the Captain's square figure she saw a shrewd-faced man, in rough homespun small-clothes and coat, with a broad-brimmed felt hat drawn low over his shaggy brows.

On Captain Knox's face shone relief and satisfaction.

"I've been most uncommon fortunate, Miss Alison," he announced, rubbing his hands together. "Mr. Ross, factor for a great man in the Mohawk country, Colonel William Johnson by name, came to inquire of me for certain goods due on the *Neptune* for his customer, from London. I asked him how I could best get you to your kinsman, and he told me that James Watson, servant to Captain Butler, was on the dock, on business for his master, and that he leaves this very afternoon for the Mohawk. So Ross, who knows him well, sent him direct to me, and

here he is. So I'll be able to put you into his care
with an easy mind. I've ordered your luggage
sent straight to the *Cheerful Polly*, the sloop
that'll carry you up Hudson River to Albany,
and from there Watson'll take you on by his
master's wagon to your journey's end. I've made
it plain to him that he's to take the best of care
of you, and to run no risks with you on the
way."

Captain Knox had said all this with scarce
pause for breath, and then, reading in the girl's
pale face how mighty an effort she was making
to keep up her brave front, he patted her shoulder encouragingly.

"Never fear, dear lass," he said, in a tone for
her ear only. " 'T will all be well. Go your ways.
There's One'll watch over you."

Alison held back the bright drops that threatened to overflow her eyes. "I doubt it not," she
answered bravely, and for a single instant she
laid her cheek confidingly on the sleeve of his
rough pea jacket, whispering her gratitude for
his care.

"There, there, 't was naught. 'T was as if I
did it for my own little maid." His voice was
husky with emotion as he told her this, and when

he added, "Good-bye, now, my brave lass, and God speed you home again."

Alison drew down his shaggy white head at that, and kissed him. "Good-bye, dear Captain Knox," she said low. One courageous smile she gave him, the first he had seen upon her face since her father left her, and then she turned to her cousin's serving-man, ready to depart.

Thick moisture bedewed the Captain's glasses, and set him to polishing them furiously as Alison followed James Watson down the companionway, across the narrow gang-plank, and so out into the streets of New York.

Chapter iv

HAVING allowed herself but one fleeting glance at the *Neptune's* bulk, where it lay with furled sails at quiet anchorage, Alison turned away, and kept close to Watson's side, as he, with her portmantle in his horny fist, wound his way in and out of the jostling throng. Not for an instant did she relax her attention to the movements of her guide, for she well knew that she would be in sore straits if she should lose sight of him.

They passed through the Meal Market, and in a corner of the enclosure she beheld, for the first time, human creatures exposed for sale— dusky slaves, with thick lips and kinky hair, their sloe-black eyes roving anxiously from side to side, while they waited to be knocked down to the highest bidder.

Clear of that gloomy spot, she found herself hurrying through a street lined with shops of pewterers, clockmakers, wigmakers, chairmakers, grocers, and inn-keepers. Each of these, with its gaily painted sign of prancing leopard, rampant unicorn, three sugar loaves and a tea-canister, mortar and pestle, dolphins, fighting cocks, or cupids, did its part to make bright the narrow thoroughfare. From the open doors of coffee-houses came the tumultuous voices of rollicking sailormen on shore leave, or countrymen come to town for trade, singing rude ditties and old-time ballads over their steaming coffee, or tankards of foaming ale.

In this neighborhood of shops and crowds she had abundant opportunity of seeing, as she followed her taciturn guide, many a richly dressed dame alighting from her sedan chair to trip daintily, in green or scarlet shoes, with satin or velvet skirt delicately lifted, into such shops as ministered to feminine vanities and necessities. She came face to face with numerous fine gentlemen, their powdered wigs neatly bound into queues, their stiff brocaded or broadcloth coats brightly colored and handsomely adorned with gold, set off with ruffles of lace and lawn, their cocked hats placed at the fashionable angle, their silver and ivory headed canes swinging jauntily as they went about their several affairs. Mingling with these were others, plainly dressed, and of lower walk in life, but not differing greatly in their garb from those of like

station in her own England. It was as John
Grayson had said: in New York they had the
fashions, and the hours spent there could be gay
enough, provided one had means and heart to
make them so.

Watson, leading her into a quieter street,
stopped before a three-storied brick house, with
small-paned windows, and dormers in its sloping
roof. It stood upon a corner, and from it a sign,
on which a black horse was crudely painted,
overhung the street. A heavy oaken door, topped
by a fan light, swung in and out at the coming
and going of its customers, for here, at the Black
Horse Tavern, favorite rendezvous of the public, and of councilmen, good entertainment was
to be had.

On the opposite side of the street, but not directly facing the hostelry was a small stationer's
shop, and between it and the house that ad-
joined it was a deep recess in the wall. To this
recess Watson directed her attention, saying, as
he broke his long silence, "You'd best wait there
for me, a bit, miss. I've business in the Black
Horse, that must be seen to before we take
sloop."

Alison looked at him in astonishment, and
gave an emphatic shake of her head. "Nay, that

I will not do," she replied. "It is not seemly that a maid should wait thus unattended upon the public street."

"'T will be but for a moment," declared Watson. "The street is quiet, as you see, and none but decent folk pass. You will come to no hurt."

Again Alison shook her head. "You must not leave me to stand alone upon the public street," she insisted.

But Watson was obstinately determined. "The place must serve," he said shortly. "I've no time to find a better, for the business is urgent, and done it must be before the *Cheerful Polly* sails at noon." Without more ado, and with her portmantle still in his hand, he strode to the tavern door, pushed it open, and disappeared from view.

So Alison was obliged to take up her position in the recess, feeling more and more conspicuous and uneasy with every passing moment in a situation so unusual to her. She stood as far back as she could in the recess, crushing herself against the rough wall, and drawing her cloak closely about her, but do what she would she felt only the more in the eye of the foot-passengers, who looked in curiously at the white face of the girl, whose gaze was fixed so anxiously upon the door of the tavern opposite.

The minutes crept on to the quarter-hour, and the quarter-hour on to the half, and still Watson had not come. Alison's perturbation increased. Could it be that Captain Butler's servant had proved faithless, and deserting her, had carried away her portmantle with him? If so, what should she do? Alone she could never make her way to the Mohawk. She began to wonder whether she dared to cast aside all maidenly precedent, and go into the tavern to seek him; to wonder, in case he should not be there, whether she had not best find her way back to the *Neptune*, and there implore Captain Knox to find some trustier escort for her, or else take her away with him on the lengthy return voyage.

In the midst of her troubled thoughts, a teasing voice smote on her ear. "Well, Mistress Gray Eyes, why do you look so eagerly toward yonder tavern? Is father, kinsman, or friend, perhaps, tarrying behind its churlish door?"

Before her stood a lad of perhaps thirteen, with a face not less striking for craft and cruelty than it was for its handsome and delicately patrician features. With hand on hip, he surveyed Alison with an impudent smile.

She, shrinking from him as he thus addressed her, gave him a glance of cold rebuff, but vouchsafed him no reply.

Her manner and action seemed to stir the youth to mischievous act. "Come, come," he persisted, catching at and pulling a loose strand of curling hair that fell from under her hood. "Let's have an answer, my maid."

Remaining silent, Alison tried to snatch free her hair, but the clutch upon it, already firm, tightened, and a second, and a sharper tweak followed hard upon the first. "Speak up, my mistress, when your betters command you," said her tormentor, tearing off her hood with a rough hand.

Alison cast a swift glance about her. Behind her, and at either side, the wall barred further retreat. Directly in front of her, blocking the entrance, and by his greater height and bulk cutting off, as she believed, all view of her from chance passersby, was this insolent youth. There seemed no possible escape from him.

In spite of that she gathered up her strength, and setting her hands hard against his chest, she tried to force him back. Her resistance only served to spur him to fresh impudence. Grasping her arms, his mocking face close to hers, he en-

aeavored to pinion her to the wall. Delicately
formed though he was, he was strong, and Alison felt herself to be no more than a reed in
his hold.

As a reed she swayed from side to side in
her violent efforts to free herself, her assailant
laughing derisively in her face meanwhile, at her
unavailing struggles.

She tried to shriek aloud for help, but smoth-
ering fright choked her voice.

Fate semed to favor the youth's rude ad-
vances, for the street was for the time deserted,
and none crossed the threshold of the tavern, nor
looked from window or door of the neighboring
houses.

Poor Alison struggling in his vise-like hold,
had come to the end of her feeble strength, when
she suddenly felt herself jerked quickly forward,
and then as abruptly liberated. Dazed and
shaken, she fell hard against the wall, breathing
heavily.

She saw a torrent of blows rained upon the
head and shoulders of her assailant; she heard an
indignant voice railing at him. A second youth
had rushed to her rescue, and while he pommeled
vigorously, he exclaimed through clenched

"*Bully! Rascal! How dare you
molest a defenceless girl!*"

teeth: "Bully! Rascal! How dare you molest a defenceless girl!"

From where she leant exhausted against the supporting wall, Alison perceived that while the first youth was by no means slow in striking back, and dodging blows, that, nevertheless, the newcomer, strong and agile, bounded away from every thrust, and sent his own blows home. At length, by a dexterous movement, he contrived to seize the girl's tormentor by the collar of his velvet coat, and shaking him to and fro like a rat, he flung him to the pavement, where he lay panting.

But presently the vanquished struggled to his feet, and casting upon his conqueror a glance in which scorn, fury, and malevolence were mingled, he strode haughtily away.

Chapter v

AS her deliverer straightened himself after the battle was finished, and the vanquished had departed, Alison had full view of his face. A brave one, and an honest it was, marked by a quick intelligence and decision. Forward-looking, clear brown eyes under level brows, nose, mouth, and chin too strong for mere beauty, there was a manliness in his countenance good to see in a youth.

His plum-colored broadcloth coat, and satin vest had been pulled awry in the struggle, one silver knee-buckle hung unfastened, his linen ruffles were jerked, and torn, and soiled. His hat, lying dented upon the ground, left bare his ruddy waving hair that glinted in the sunshine. A lad he was that Alison knew that she must have liked heartily on sight, even had he not just done her such signal service.

She found her voice. " 'T is a great debt that I owe you," she stammered blushing, "and one that I can never repay."

"Speak not of it," he returned. " 'T was joy

to trounce such an unmannerly villain for you."
His face rekindled with indignation at the memory of the scene that he had come upon. Bending, he readjusted his knee-buckles, put right his
disordered coat and vest, picked up his hat,
pressed out the dent in its crown, and was about
to depart; but the little maid standing lonely
against the wall stirred him to further speech.
"He got not the half of his deserts," he blurted
out. "I would I had drubbed the ruffian yet more
soundly."

"He has good cause to remember what you
gave him," observed Alison gravely.

"It pleases me to believe it." Once more he
essayed to go, yet still he tarried. "Were I so
fair a maid as you," he advised her sagely, "I
would not risk further impertinence by standing there."

Alison flushed hotly. She was loth to have this
gallant stranger believe that she would loiter
alone upon the street from choice. "I thought
to have been gone long since," she made haste to
explain, "but he who has the care of me bade
me await him here."

"He guards you somewhat ill," was the quick
comment. "Lest you meet with more effrontery,
I will bide with you till he comes."

But there was no need that he should tarry, for at that moment the door of the Black Horse Tavern swung open, and James Watson emerged.

"I thank you much," said Alison shyly to her self-elected protector, "but yonder he comes."

The lad, following the direction of her eyes, assured himself that he might safely leave her, and, bowing, gave her good morning.

Watson, engrossed in placing a folded paper in the inner pocket of his coat, reached Alison before he raised his head, and when he did so he saw nothing that apprised him of her misadventure, so fully had she restored to neatness her apparel and her tumbled hair.

He made no excuses for his prolonged absence. "We'll be on our way now, miss," he began. "You'll be needing a bit of dinner soon, but that's to be had on the sloop. She lies by the dock at Quincy's Market, on Hudson River. We'll be there in short enough time."

It was a pleasant way by which he led her, and as they walked briskly along Alison was almost insensibly diverted from the memory of her late disagreeable encounter by the interest of what she saw. On either side of the street were well-built and handsome houses, some in

the quaint Dutch style, and some in the English,
and one and all were surrounded by delightsome
gardens. The brick pavements were softly
shaded by forest trees, and were bordered by
velvet grass. Through the open fences she
glimpsed springing violets, pale crocuses, and
flaunting of gay tulips.

Although in her forlorn state she made no
part of it, she felt the sweetness of its atmos-
phere of homes, and happy wholesome life, but
presently, in passing the low hall of Trinity
churchyard, she saw that which brought her sorrow freshly to mind. The sunlight, filtering
through the leaves, spread itself like a benison
over many a green mound and lifted headstone.
By one of these stood a group of young girls,
clad in white, each holding a flower-filled basket
in her hand. According to the springtime custom
of old New York they had come there to strew
blossoms on the grave of a lost companion. In
voices low-toned and sweet they sang together:

"Let her have fair flowers enough,
  White and purple, green and yellow,
For her that was of maids most true,
  For her that was of maids most true."

Remembering a lonely grave far out at sea,
over which the hoarse voices of the waves were

lifted, Alison turned her eyes away in haste from the peaceful sunny spot, and put stern check upon herself.

Thinking of her father, she was suddenly reminded of his last charge, and instinctively her hand went to her bosom, to make sure that the packet that he had given her was still securely lodged there. To her consternation it was gone.

With a sharp exclamation of dismay, she began to make hurried search for it, but her trembling fingers quickly assured her that it was indeed gone, and she guessed, with a stab at her heart, that it had fallen out unobserved while she struggled with her annoyer. At no other time could its loss have passed unnoticed.

Watson, a few paces ahead of her, did not hear her cry of distress. Alison rushed forward, and caught him by the arm.

"Stop! Stop!" she entreated. "I have lost something of great value. We must go back at once, and seek it."

The serving-man halted grudgingly, for the time was growing short, and he had just been congratulating himself that Quincy's Market, where the Albany sloops cast anchor, and where the *Cheerful Polly* was moored, was now at no great distance.

"What's it you've lost?" demanded he.

"A packet," she told him in a shaking voice. "A packet of much import, that my father bade me give to Captain Butler. Oh come," she begged piteously, wringing her hands. "Come quickly, lest it be lost to me altogether."

Watson dared not deny her. He turned, albeit ungraciously, and they began to retrace their steps. His small shrewd eyes, and her large troubled ones scanned every inch of the clean-swept pavements as they went, but in vain. Arrived at the embrasure in the wall, they made most diligent and thorough search in its neighborhood, and failing there also, they inquired in the near-by shops, in case anyone had found it, and left it to be claimed by its owner. Watson stepped into the Black Horse, to see if it might be there, and finding that it was not, he posted a notice of its loss, with a promise of reward for its return.

Once more they set out for the sloop, Alison silent and overwhelmed with distress, and James Watson none too easy in his mind, for during their search Alison had recounted what had happened to her during his absence in the tavern.

By dint of much haste they reached the sloop before she drew anchor, and Alison went on board, and took refuge in the tiny stateroom that Watson, with some difficulty, had managed to secure for her. In its welcome privacy she sat down to painful thought.

The contents of the packet were unknown to her, but she knew that her fortunes were bound up in it. As to the letter—how was she to establish her kinship without it? With packet and letter she had felt that her welcome was assured. Without them, how would Captain Butler receive her? Child though she was, she did not fail to realize how grave was her present situation, and the more she thought of it, the graver it seemed.

Pale of face, with wide unseeing eyes, she sat upon the edge of her berth in miserable discomfort. The little vessel held its course past low shores, frowning palisades, bold headlands, and promontories, but she was conscious of them only as vague shapes that slipped by like ghosts. When Watson summoned her to food, she went, and ate mechanically, but returned as quickly as she could to her solitude, and to her anxious thoughts.

Day after day she passed in the same fashion, except when driven by need of air and exercise to a pacing of the narrow deck, or to a seat in some corner where she could be withdrawn from the gaze of passengers and deck-hands. Watson saw to her needs, but outside of these left her to her own devices.

Meanwhile she was traveling on the bosom of a noble and majestic stream that widened to a great bay at the Tappan Zee before it narrowed to wind through channels of dream-like beauty: channels that at first glance ended abruptly against mountain sides, offering no outlet, yet always opening mysteriously to lead on to yet more verdant slopes, and tremendous steeps that thrust out their wooded spurs as if to guard and bar the way. High Tor's bold front, Bear Mountain's bulk, the profile of Anthony's Nose (as yet unnamed for Mad Anthony), the small sharp cone of Sugar Loaf, Storm King a crouching lion, Mount Beacon with its companioning heights, how these would have delighted her, seen under happier circumstances, but now, these, together with wide glimpses across open country to the far blue hills of Connecticut, had no other significance than that of objects that must be passed.

On and up the river went the sturdy little sloop, until the Catskills had been left behind, and they drew in to the little city of Albany after ten days of voyaging.

It was not until the night before the *Cheerful Polly* moored at her dock, that any lightening of her misery came to Alison. Then, though it was vouchsafed her in a dream only, it brought marvelous comfort to her overburdened heart. It was as though she stood alone on the bank of a swiftly moving stream, thick strewn with sharp and cruel rocks and treacherous bars of shifting sand. Still quite alone, she was obliged to cross to the other side, and the bark which lay near, and to which she must trust herself to be borne over the waters, was alarmingly frail. Looking upon it, she shuddered, and could not bring herself to put foot in the tossing craft.

While she stood, hesitant and trembling, her father appeared at her side, tall and strong, reassuring and loving, as he had always been to her in life. He took her in his arms and kissed her with an inexpressible tenderness, and she heard his voice ring clear. "Go forward, my dear, my brave laddie-lass. The Lord is with you. There will be safe crossing."

With his words still sounding in her ears, she awoke. His "brave laddie-lass," yes, that she must be. She would go forward, and trust.

Chapter vi

IN the heavy farm wagon that had come to meet James Watson at the dock, Alison jolted through the quiet streets of Albany, past neat Dutch houses of red and black Holland brick, set gable-end to the street. Her eyes were caught by the oddly curving roofs, corbel-edged, and surmounted by weather vanes in the forms of prancing lions, horses, sloops in full sail, or crowing cocks, strangely different in appearance from the housetops of Kent.

The dew still glistened on the trim gardens, beginning to be gay with flowering shrubs, and spring bloom. Set close to the garden beds were rows of thriving young vegetables such as those she knew. A flock of snowy geese waddled importantly away to seek the water, and down the broad well-paved street lined with button-wood trees, she saw the town cowherd with his horn, driving the cows, musical with tinkling bells, to pasture them outside the town walls.

Blue sky overhead, swiftly moving banners of

white cloud, a crisp fresh air, lifted Alison's
spirits. Who could be altogether buried in sad-
ness when Springtime's magic wand was lifted
over the land?

A low murmur of conversation came to her
steadily from the rough seat of the wagon where
Watson sat beside Pieter Brouck, the driver.
Erect upon a low bench which had been placed
for her, together with her baggage, in the center
of the vehicle, she could catch only a chance
word here and there. The talk was of beaver-
skins, the price of flour, and other articles of
merchandise, and these interested her not at all.

On creaked the heavy wagon through the
home-like little town, past the rude fort, past
the curiously built church, past a company of
chattering boys with rods and guns and hampers,
and girls with workbaskets, bound upon one of
those early morning picnics by the river so pop-
ular among the youth of Albany in colonial days.

Coming soon out upon the good highroad that
led over hill and dale toward Schenectady, she
saw, placed as closely and sociably along it as
the boundaries of their respective farmsteads
would permit, one tidy comfortable Dutch house
after another. Perched on a hilltop, to catch the
benefit of every passing breeze, a windmill with

steadily turning sails was making ready the flour for the housewives' ovens.

Occasionally a farmer jogged by them in his cart, or a youth and maid riding pillion trotted past, but the dust raised by wheels and hoofs made so thick a cloud around them as to half hide them from view. Wrapping her cloak closer about her, she pulled her traveling hood over her face to guard herself from the stifling dust.

She had no sooner done this, when on a sudden two horsemen, like twin meteors, burst through the yellow haze, galloping furiously.

The first was an officer in the scarlet uniform of the British army. His mount, coal black and powerful, betrayed by his frothing mouth and foam-flecked sides how he was goaded by bit and spur.

Directly behind him, on a bright bay, all a-lather, rode a youth, whom, in the brief glimpse she had of him, Alison recognized as the one who had made himself obnoxious to her before the Black Horse Tavern. Never could she be mistaken in that cruelly handsome face and scornful bearing.

They were gone in a flash, but not before the girl, fearful lest she should be seen, and recognized in her turn, had slipped down from her seat to crouch in the straw that lined the wagon-bed. There, with hood caught yet closer to conceal her face, with every nerve and muscle tense with anxiety, she watched the two until they had disappeared below the crest of the hill. Then she drew free breath once more, and resumed her seat upon the bench.

As the riders swept across her own vision, she was conscious that James Watson, seeing them also, had given a start of surprise and recognition. But the horsemen, with faces set straight forward, did not so much as glance at the wagon and its occupants.

"Whew! There's none rides so fast as Colonel John, and his son, and none so hard on horse-flesh!" she heard Watson exclaim to his companion. "They go it like the devil himself!"

"Dot iss so," nodded the other, "und sometimes I tink dey be deffils."

Their voices dropped to a cautious undertone, and during the remainder of the fifteen miles that divided them from Schenectady Alison heard only the monotonous rumble of the cart wheels, the creaking of the axle, and the indistinguishable murmurings of the men.

Thus far upon her journey she had seen no redskins, although she had been prepared to encounter them at almost any moment since she left the *Neptune*, but in their progress through the quiet peaceful towns, and between the broad well-tilled fields on either side of the road she had marked none but Dutch or English faces.

Beyond the fields lay wild dense forests and towering rugged heights. Hidden among these she knew not what might lurk, either of savage beasts, or wigwams or lodges of equally savage human kind. Tales she had heard by her own safe fireside in England of settlers dwelling in fancied security among their Indian neighbors, only to be descended upon swiftly, treacherously, brutally; and annihilation by hatchet, tomahawk, and firebrand had followed, leaving only ashes and embers to mark the spot where happy homes had stood, and hearthfires burned.

A backless bench, and a springless wagon proved none too comfortable to a tenderly reared maid like Alison, and when the driver drew rein before a clean but unpretentious inn at Schenectady, where they were to change horses, and refresh themselves with a hot meal, she was glad enough to alight, and stretch her stiffened knees by pacing up and down the inn parlor, while James Watson ordered dinner, and Pieter Brouck gossiped with the hostler.

Made keenly hungry by her long ride in the fresh morning air, she answered the summons to table, when it came, with alacrity.

The men fell to voraciously upon the steaming hodge-pot that was set before them, washing it down with copious draughts of brown ale. Their heads bent over the table, they were oblivious to everything except the satisfaction of appetite.

Alison, however, facing the open door, and taking her food more daintily than they, presently became aware of a human figure standing just outside the threshold, and looking in. She raised her eyes quickly, and beheld a savage, his face copper-hued in the blaze of the noon-day sun.

He was clad from head to foot in doeskin. From his belt hung glittering knife, stone tomahawk, and keen-edged hatchet. A single tuft of jet black hair stood upright on his scalp above his mask-like visage. His eyes, of a piercing blackness, were fixed upon the group at table.

Her flesh creeping at this hideous apparition, Alison choked back the shriek that rose to her throat, and clutched James Watson by the sleeve.

"See, see yonder!" she gasped. "In the door-way!"

Watson, his knife filled with hominy, suddenly arrested halfway between plate and mouth, turned his head toward the door, but found it empty.

"What was't you saw, miss?" he asked in surprise.

"A savage," breathed Alison, dry-lipped, "a savage, most fierce, and horrible!"

James Watson uttered a short laugh, and laid down his knife, for at that same instant in which she spoke there came from without a low mournful sound like the cry of an owl at nightfall.

"'T is Hooting Owl, the Caughnawaga," he said, and rose abruptly. "He is a friend, and wants speech with me. Stay you here at dinner, miss, with Pieter Brouck."

Without further ado he left the inn.

Perceiving that neither he nor Pieter showed signs of alarm at the proximity of this formidable-looking savage, Alison struggled back to outward composure, but she could eat no more.

In a little while Watson came back, finished his meal hastily, and then went to pay the reckoning. Pieter took himself off to make sure that sufficiently sturdy horses were being put to the wagon to carry them to the end of their journey.

Left to await their return, Alison went to the window, and looked out. The small well-polished panes commanded a view of the narrow street that led to the fort, a little distance away.

As her eyes took in the details of this rude bulwark of protection against marauding savages, and possible invasion by Frenchmen from the north, she saw a groom lead out a pair of fiery horses, and bring them to a stand at the fortress gate.

Sauntering after him, talking to a little group of fellow officers, came the scarlet-uniformed rider who had passed her in the dust. At his heels was the youth who had companioned him.

Alison drew back hastily from the window, yet placed herself so that she could still see, but without being seen. It filled her with dismay to find that she continued to possess so unwelcome a neighbor, and she was eager to learn the direction that the two would take. With all her heart she hoped that they would be well away, before she must herself go forth.

In this she had her desire. They tarried but for a last jovial sally with the officers of the fort, and then, vaulting into their saddles, took reins, buried their spurs deep into the flanks of their fretful horses, and pounded away along the road that led westward.

Although they had gone in the direction in which she knew she, too, must proceed, the girl breathed more freely after their departure, and she was quite willing to climb again into the wagon at Watson's summons.

Rumbling past the fort, with its rough masonry of stones, and piled timbers, its four bastions, and its cannon-guarded ramparts, she thought, with relief, that those whom she had seen lately issuing from this great, raised gate were already too far in advance of her to make it likely that she would encounter them again.

At a short distance from the outskirts of the little town they came to the bank of a river. It was the Mohawk, winding its lovely length from west to east between blue hills and low green flats, and dotted throughout its course with innumerable richly wooded islands.

A clumsy ferry lay close to shore, and stretched full length upon its deck, napping in the sun, was the ferryman.

Pieter Brouck gave him a hail. "Ho, ho! Jan Peek! Vake oop, und dake us ofer."

The sleepy Dutchman rubbed his eyes, and

got him deliberately to his feet, for he was a man of great girth, and hence not one to hasten over-much.

"Vell, vell, Pieter Brouck! You gotten back, ain't it?" he observed placidly. "Pring on shteady now. Right in mittle. So-o-o."

The wagon lumbered onto the ferry. The horses stood. With a strong deft shove of the ferryman's pole they were away from land, and moving across water. Deliberate and slow as the ferryman himself, the heavy raft bore its freight to the opposite shore, and there debarked it.

Jan Peek received his fare in his enormous palm, and under his solemn ox-like gaze the horses, with a tugging and straining at their traces, struggled up the bank.

Once more began the jolt, jolt, jolt of the wagon, the monotonous creaking of the axle, the rising clouds of dust; and as before James Watson and Pieter Brouck droned away in unintelligible undertones, leaving the weary girl to solitude and her own thoughts.

Twilight was drawing on, and still they journeyed. Alison, aching in every limb, was beginning to feel as though the long ride would never be over. Farther down the road, and set close to it was a spacious stone mansion with many clustered outbuildings. A merry creek, the Kayaderosseros, rushed beside it, busily turning a mill, and the pleasant sound of falling water, the cooing of pigeons in a near-by dove-cote, the sweet odor of baking bread from the bake-house ovens, stirred Alison to the hope that this might be their journey's end. But instead of turning in at the neat driveway, Pieter Brouck only touched his whip to the plodding horses, and they had jolted by.

Up and up a long steep hill, and slowly down again, with the valley growing every moment lovelier in the fading light, and then they turned away from the main road to mount a second, and much lonelier incline, that rose with such abruptness that the horses could with difficulty make the ascent. Alison was obliged to cling tightly to her seat, and at length to sit flat down upon the floor of the wagon, for between the jarring caused by the stones and dried ruts, and the steepness of the rising ground she had been dangerously near to being spilled out upon the road.

The top reached, they turned to the right, and went a few rods further. An open gate gave entrance to a farm road, which led straight to a low wooden house set on a commanding height.

Encircled by forest trees, its sharply pointed

roof sloping at one side almost to the ground, its weathered shingles and unpainted walls showing gray in the thickening dusk, it seemed to the travel-worn little maid a gloomy and solitary abode enough.

Pieter Brouck brought his horses to a stand before its closed door. Watson climbed down from the wagon, and Alison, with a sinking of the heart, took his offered hand, and clambered down over the wheel.

"Here ye be, miss," said Watson, and led her to the door. "Come right along of me, but you'd best let me have first word with the master."

The opening door gave into a narrow hallway, and in the room to the left a fire glowed. With Alison close following, Watson went directly to it, and he having tapped upon the door-frame, they entered at the bidding of a voice from within.

In a huge armchair, by the wide stone fireplace, basking his limbs in the heat that streamed from the half-burned logs, sat an aged man, swathed in a dressing-gown of dull puce-colored velvet, snuff-stained and faded. A skull cap of black silk covered his poll, and made his pale face appear more waxen, his sharply cut features more severely cold than any that Alison had ever seen heretofore. His thin hands clutched the arms of his chair as claws might. Eyes dark and piercing still, despite his more than eighty years, turned themselves upon the travelers with an imperious frown. Thin lips, that seemed strangers to kindly speech, were closed above a determined and unrelenting chin.

Truly, in the person of this man, Captain Walter Butler, there was scant hope that poor Alison would find gentle guardianship.

Yet that which struck cold fear and mortal distress to the heart of the poor orphaned maid was not, after all, this forbidding figure of a stern old man, but his companions, for seated near him, the one with his glance fixed upon her in haughty surprise and inquiry, the other with a flash of recognition and mockery in his eyes, were the scarlet-coated officer, seen for the first time in the morning of this day, and the delicate-featured youth, whom she had seen on the day of her landing from the *Neptune*, and had such just cause to detest and dread.

Chapter vii

FOR an instant there was dead silence in the room. Then Captain Butler, leaning forward in his chair, fixed an angry eye upon James Watson. "Who's yonder jade?" he demanded.

Watson found his tongue. "A young English miss, sent to you by the captain of the *Neptune*, sir. She claims to be kin of yours; but the young miss will speak for herself, no doubt."

"That I will," said Alison quietly, in spite of the furious beating of her heart, and stepped out of the shadow. The shock that she had sustained on entering, at seeing these three together, and to find, as their singular likeness to one another clearly indicated, that they were of the same strain, had in some measure passed. In all she marked the same hauteur, in varying degree the same coldly cruel lip and jaw, the same scornful brow and eye, and from them she knew that she need expect no kindness.

But the very hardship of her position served as a spur to her. That courage, deep within her,

which her father had been wont to praise, rose
to her aid. Target though she was for all their
eyes, she held herself straight with lifted head.

"I am no jade," she began, with a simple dignity not common in one so young. "I am Alison
Blair. Your cousin, Alison Doane, was wife to
my father, Dr. Matthew Blair."

At the name, Captain Butler scanned the girl
narrowly. He remembered perfectly that he had
had a young relative, Alison Doane, but she had
been a child when he last saw her, a child in Ireland. And now, forsooth, by an impudent stretching of the tie of blood, a daughter of hers had
crossed the sea to present herself at his door, perhaps to beseech his charity: but she would
quickly learn that his house was not a shelter for
all his needy kin.

Under the harshness of the old man's scrutiny,
Alison had paused, and before she could speak
again, he had flung at her: "What brings you
here? Make the tale a short one."

"My father's wish, and my own necessity,"
replied Alison, turning herself half away from
sight of the youth, who was watching her with a
sardonic smile. "Coming with me to the Colonies
on the ship *Neptune*, my father was suddenly
killed by a sailor who had gone mad. Dying, he

thought of you, and bade the captain send me to you."

"To seek my charity, I suppose," broke in Captain Butler sourly. "He had done better to send you packing back to England, where you belong." This he said, striking his palm hard upon his broad chair-arm.

"It was to England that he meant to have me go, but not without safe conduct," declared the girl, her cheeks burning hotly at the insult of his tone. "And 't was this he meant that I should ask you to obtain for me, and shelter till it could be found. This, and no more."

"You had but to stay upon the *Neptune* to get you back to England, and there your mother could have fetched you from the vessel," was the tart reply.

"My mother is long since dead, and the *Neptune* makes a voyage of well-nigh a year before she touches England again," said Alison. "It was not by choice of my own that I came here. I but obeyed my father and Captain Knox, I being a friendless maid, and alone in the land."

Her voice was a shade unsteady, in spite of herself, as she said this, but there was no note of sympathy in that of Captain Butler as he returned, "Of this Captain Knox, who tries to

foist you off upon me, I know nothing nor of
Matthew Blair. As to my kinswoman, Alison
Doane, before I believe you to be child of hers,
you must show proof of it."

Alison winced. Proof enough she could give
when her own and her father's chest were laid
open that she was daughter to Matthew Blair,
and that he was a gentleman and a physician,
but she had none to show that she was child of
Alison Doane. Mayhap such proof had been
among the papers in the packet that she had
lost, but the packet being gone, she had but her
bare word to offer.

"And your passage money? You have that
with you?" pursued Captain Butler coldly. "For
surely you would scarce have sufficient impudence to expect me to defray that for you."

"Be not too sure of that, grandsir," cut in
young Walter Butler, from his seat beside his
father, Colonel John. "Had you seen the forward behavior of this girl upon the streets of
New York, as did I, you would know her for a
hussy, and be prepared for anything."

Stung to the quick at this outrageous falsehood, Alison faced him accusingly. "When I remember," she declared, "how you set upon and
insulted there a defenceless maid, who did but

stand modestly and quietly in what seemed a sheltered spot, waiting for the return of the one who had left her there, and into whose protection she had been given, I am not surprised that you should lie thus concerning me. 'T is the second time you have done me foul wrong."

Walter Butler threw back his head, and laughed insolently. "Of that you have as much proof," he retorted, "as that you are my grandsir's kin."

Alison set her back to him, and again addressed the old man. "If Captain Knox were here, sir, you would know him to be an honest man, and he would tell you of my father, and of me. Indeed, I had a letter which my poor father writ you in his last hour, and this he sent to you by me, together with a packet, that I know contained papers of value, if not monies."

At the mention of papers of value, Colonel John Butler, who, until now, had lolled in his chair, scarlet-clad legs indolently crossed, listening to the girl's story with cynical indifference, sat bolt upright. After all, this might be a true tale! As for young Walter, boys would be boys, and doubtless the insult of which she made so great a matter was but some teasing act of his, too trifling to take note of. One could never tell what a maid would make a to-do about. But *papers of value*—that was another thing, and worthy of serious attention.

Into the dusky eyes of the old man shrewd avarice leapt. If this girl had papers of value, be she kin or no, he was not loth to look them over. One thin hand gripped the chair-arm yet more closely. The other he extended peremptorily to Alison. "If you have papers of value to be given to my charge," he commanded, "produce them."

Across the countenance of young Walter flitted the ghost of a smile.

"I have them no longer," replied Alison, with quivering lip. "They were safe hidden in my breast, until this rude fellow attacked me. After he was gone I missed them, and they must have fallen out while I struggled to free myself from him."

"A lie," scoffed Walter to his grandfather. "Had what she says been true, she would have seen the packet lying upon the ground, and would have recovered it instantly."

"It is no lie," protested Alison indignantly. "At no other time could I have lost them, although I did not miss them at the first, nor indeed until I drew near the sloop. Then it was too late to find them, but your serving-man can tell you how we went back again, and searched for them."

Captain Butler wheeled to Watson. "Well, what do you know of this?" he growled. Watson revolved his hat slowly in his hands while he gave cautious answer. "Only that just before we reached the *Cheerful Polly* this young miss cried out that she had lost papers and a letter, and must go back and hunt for them." His words were true enough, but there was that in his tone that made Alison, listening tensely, know that he would trim his sails to suit the wind.

"Captain Knox had said nothing to you, James, concerning these papers?" queried Captain Butler.

"No, sir. Nothing of the sort," was the reply.

"'T was not his business to know of them," spoke Alison.

"And this girl waited until you had well-nigh reached the sloop before she began to bewail her loss?" scoffed the old man, ignoring Alison's speech. "Bah! She cut her story from the whole cloth between the tavern and the sloop. Had she been annoyed upon the street she would have bawled it out for all to hear. Had she met with loss, she would not have been so long in discovering it and telling you of it."

"That might be, sir," granted Watson deferentially, "but all I know of her is what Captain Knox told me, and I was bid by him to bring her here to you."

"You should have known your duty better, Watson, than to take up any such commission," put in Colonel John Butler importantly. "With a wench on his hands to be disposed of somehow, Captain Knox has made a catspaw of you."

"Ay, that he has, sir," admitted the servingman, shifting himself uneasily from one foot to the other.

Alison shot him a glance of reproach, which he feigned not to see.

"And by Gad, if I know my father," continued the officer, chopping out his words rapidly, "she, with her tale of insults from my son, and lost papers, and talk of kin, has brought her wares to the wrong market."

"That she has," agreed old Butler, emphatically. "She'll not foist herself off upon me. Kin, forsooth—and if she were, what was Alison Doane to me, that I should house and feed her brat?"

Finding herself denied and repudiated by the one to whom she had been sent for protection, and made aware that she need hope for no support of claims by Watson, Alison's heart sank low in her breast. She found herself, indeed, in hard case.

Young Walter, at no pains to conceal his enjoyment of her situation, was eager to add one more sting to it. "If what you said of me had been true," he mocked at her, " 't is strange that you should seek now to prove yourself my cousin."

"Had I known that you were here," cried Alison, turning blazing eyes upon him, "you may be sure 't is the last place to which I should have been willing to come."

"Willing or not willing," snarled Captain Butler, fiercely, "it is not the place where you'll stay. Out with you, baggage. Out, with your lies, and your impudent face. Open the door, Watson. Put her over the threshold—by force, if she won't go otherwise."

So brutal was the command that Alison doubted that she could have heard aright. But under James Watson's obedient hand the door was already swinging open into the night. The wind, damp now, and penetrating, rushed in.

There was neither moon nor star to break the inky blackness that lay outside.

Aghast at this sudden turn of fate, the girl shuddered; not alone with the chill that struck her body, but with the leaping dread of hideous dangers that doubtless lay beyond the warm shelter of the house walls under cover of the night.

Ruthless these Butlers were; evidently without mercy, or faintest touch of human feeling, but she feared them infinitely less than she did the vast wild spaces without, where savages lurked, and deeds of blood were done.

"Oh, surely," she cried, and there was a high note of terror in her voice, "you would not cast me forth at night to the mercy of savages!"

"Yes, to the mercy of savages," jeered Walter, gloating upon the anguish of her face. "You'll learn what that means, and before long."

But it was as if Alison did not hear this lesser voice. Her fate, so it seemed to her, lay in the power of the octogenarian, wrapped in his somber robe. It was to him that she must plead, must make him listen to her, must compel him to a mercy foreign to him.

She crept nearer to him, and wrung her

hands in an agony of entreaty, that might have moved a heart of flint. "Oh, I beseech you," she exclaimed, "do not treat me so cruelly. Let me have shelter at least until the morning."

"This is no tavern, wench," was the curt reply; and then to his serving-man, "James, you had my orders. Obey them."

James Watson approached Alison to take her by force. But she darted from him like a hunted thing.

Young Walter, with vengeful delight over her frantic despair, sat watching her speed from one apparent refuge to another, while Watson, less agile than she, pursued her with stolid determination, cutting off her avenues of escape one by one, narrowing her down.

The old man, with pitiless gaze, his son, with a mien as grim, marked her every movement. They sat, these three, silently following with their eyes the hunter and the hunted, as though it were some choice spectacle, arranged as of set purpose for their malevolent enjoyment.

To the farthest corner of the room rushed Alison, to delay, even if by ever so little, the dread moment when she should be thrust out. In her desperate strait a wild shriek burst from her lips. "Oh, father, father, had you known

this, you would have sent me to a den of lions
sooner!"

"Even in the lion's den, little one," answered
a voice, unheard till now. "the Lord takes care
of His own."

Chapter viii

IT was a woman who spoke: a woman, tall, and strong, and fair. In her comely face strength of mind and purpose held equal sway with a large and fine serenity. Dressed after the gay fashion of the Dutch housewives of her time, in purple worsted skirt, striped bodice, crisp white cap with wing-like tabs, crisp apron, crisply gathered sleeves, both white as her cap, Maria Butler entering by a door set close to the corner to which Alison had retreated, was to the eyes of the poor overwrought child as a very angel of deliverance sent down to succor her where she crouched at bay.

It was as an angel might, that the good woman raised the trembling girl, and gathered her to the safety of her breast.

"Listen to me, you Butlers of the hard hearts," she said, in ringing voice, "this child goes not out into the night. No, not while Maria Wemple lives to shield her from you. I have heard what you have been saying to her, and

2

each new word made you blacker yet than the last one. From the oldest of you to the youngest you show yourselves alike. You have denied this poor little one, and given to her the lie; but I believe her, and will take care of her. Not tonight, nor tomorrow yet, shall she go forth unless she wills it, and when she goes, she shall go in good hands."

Colonel John Butler shifted uneasily in his chair. Walter all at once became absorbed in the glowing logs that had fallen asunder, and rising grasped tongs to lay them close again. But the old man glared upon her.

"Who gives you leave to rule here, Maria Butler?" he thundered in hot anger. "This house is mine, and my will is the law of it."

"Maria Butler I became, it is true, when I married my good husband, your son Wat, and for his sake I left a house where decent kindness is to be found, to come where there is none. But Maria Wemple I am in blood, and ways, and spirit, and so I will remain. In this house I am not without rights, for I did not come to it with empty hands, and when justice calls me to speak, my voice will be heard with respect by you even."

Each word fell from her lips with quiet meas-

ured force. There was no flush upon her broad
kindly face, nor ruffling of her wide smooth
brow, but there was mastery in her very presence.

"You say she is not of kin to you," she continued, stroking with soothing touch the tumbled
curls on Alison's bowed head. "And what of
that? She is a homeless child, of need most bitter. She shall stay with me, then, until she can
be got home again, and we shall see who will
dare to raise the hand against her."

Walter laid down the tongs, and spread his
fingers lazily toward the rising flames. "As a
serving-maid she may, of course, be useful to
you," he insinuated to his aunt. "It would be a
fitting place for her in this household." He cast
a glance at Alison from under his lowered brows,
that he might catch some sign that his gibe had
struck home.

"You bring your son up ill, John Butler,"
commented Mistress Maria calmly, turning her
placid gaze upon his father. "Teach him to curb
his tongue, ay, and his manners, too, while he
is under this roof." And then to Alison, "Come,
child, with me. Of these, thou'st already had too
much. Watson, make shut the door, that we get
not such strong night wind in the house."

Glad enough was Alison to follow whither her conductress led. Like a storm-tossed bird that has unexpectedly found safe haven, she came to the comfort of the great kitchen. There she sank down, still white and shaken, upon a wide oaken settle, placed cosily at right angles to the yawning fireplace.

Savory odors, escaping from the covered iron pots swung upon massive cranes over the piled embers, floated to her nostrils. A negro wench, half seen through the open buttery door, was carving slabs from a huge round cheese. The steady ticking of the Dutch clock upon the wall could be plainly heard above the crackle of the logs, the bubbling of the soup, and the hissing of the fat falling from the roasting meat upon the turning spit into the dripping-pan below.

Too faint and unstrung, as yet, by the perils that had lately beset her, too dazed by the blessed miracle of her rescue to take more note of the details of her present surroundings than to be sensible of the peaceful shelter that they afforded her, she leaned against the high back of the settle, with drooped head, and half-closed eyes, content merely to be quiet.

In the fire-glow that flooded the room to its uttermost corners, Mistress Butler moved, a reassuring, protecting presence, and to the weary girl that was quite enough.

But Maria Butler knew that more than rest alone was needed. She filled a pewter porringer with soup from the cauldron, cut and spread with butter a slice of bread from the fresh brown loaf, and came with them to sit beside Alison on the settle.

"Come, my little one, come kleintje, thou must have this. It will give back the strength again. See, I will feed thee, and when thou hast finished, thou shalt have thy bed."

Obediently Alison took the food as it was dealt out to her, and under the stimulant of the hot fluid, Mistress Butler saw color steal slowly back to the pale cheeks.

When the last drop had been swallowed, and the last morsel also, her kind protectress rose, and set aside the porringer, and horn spoon. "Thou hast done well," she commended.

She took up a heavy iron candlestick, and lighted the tallow candle with a pine splinter kindled at the hearth.

"Now to thy bed," said she, and beckoned to the stair.

A little room, a peaceful room it was to which she led Alison when they had climbed to the up-

per floor. The flickering rays of the candle
showed quaintly sloping walls, a neat bed, piled
high with snowy pillows inviting to repose, an
oaken chest of drawers whose polished surfaces
twinkled a welcome, a many-hued rag rug upon
the bare scoured boards, a window looking
through pine boughs to a rising moon.

"Here, without anxiousness, thou mayst
rest," Mistress Butler assured her. "Look. To
the door there is a bar. It is thus that thou must
use it. In the next room I myself sleep. If thou
hast fear in the night, tap upon this wall, and
I will come."

Alison thanked her dumbly with her eyes.

Going to the chest of drawers, Maria Butler
took out a clean nightdress and shook out its
ample folds. "'T is large for thee," she smiled,
"but for tonight it will serve."

Alison tried to voice the gratitude that welled
up from her full heart.

"Kleintje, speak of it not at all," Maria bade
her. "Thou owest me nothing. I could have done
no less and have right to be called a woman."

She encircled the girl with maternal arms,
and kissed her forehead. "Surely thou dost need
a friend, poor child, and in Maria Butler thou
hast one; and shalt have one in my Wat, too,

when he comes home from Schenectady and I tell him of this."

Then she left her, and Alison dropped the sturdy bar to place, with a welcome sense of security.

Slipping off her clothes, she donned the homespun linen garment that Mistress Butler had provided. It engulfed her.

Blowing out the candle, she crept to the bedside, and knelt down to her evening prayer. Now that all restraint was lifted, and she was quite alone with God, there came sob after sob in place of words, and a rush of long-checked tears. "I am not brave," she wept, "for indeed, indeed, I am but a lass."

The sound of her weeping she smothered with the coverlet, lest those who hated her should overhear and take pleasure in her grief, and lest she who had befriended her should be distressed for her.

Never had she so longed for her father; never had he seemed so remote from her, and consoled though she had been by Maria Butler's kindness and protection, she told herself that she was but one, while her enemies were thrice the number.

Barred in this tiny room, she was safe for a night, but in the morning she must arise, and go forth of it, to meet she knew not what. Therefore in helplessness and loneliness of spirit she gave way to bitter weeping.

Yet not for long. Soon she found herself praying earnestly, though almost without speech, with an intense going up of her soul to the Father of the fatherless, and praying thus, her loneliness was lifted, and she could rise from her knees at last, and lie down in her bed comforted, to fall into a dreamless sleep.

Chapter ix

THE morning sun, making its way through the fragrant screen of pine boughs, awoke Alison.

Somewhere, out of sight, a robin sang full-throated greeting to the day, a care-free out-pouring, as though proclaiming that the world was not dark but bright, and that there was safety to be found in the midst of danger.

Alison arose, and stole to the window, to see if she could catch sight of this cheering neighbor, but he was too well concealed. Instead she glimpsed a flash of scarlet on the roadway that led to the Indian country beyond, and a sound of hoofbeats growing faint, and fainter, in the distance. It was Colonel John Butler, traveling home to his command at Fort Hunter.

Hoping that she might descry his son accompanying him, she strained eyes and ears until some time after he had disappeared among the trees that lined the hill-road, but none followed him.

Disappointed as she was at this, it comforted

her not a little that she was to have one less hostile presence to encounter when she should descend the stair.

She stood a moment longer, looking out upon the valley, that stretched away in exquisite beauty far below the lofty hilltop on which the Butler house was set. Dark blue heights, rocky bluffs, primeval forests, and fields of waving corn bordered the bright waters of the Mohawk River, which lay, a sheet of polished silver, under the swiftly rising sun. Opalescent mist cast a delicate haze over the spring green, and draped itself like a veil of gossamer over the blossoming apple and peach trees in the orchard. From unseen nests arose gentle twitterings.

It was well-nigh impossible for the girl to believe, on this fair morning, with the soft air touching her cheek like a caress, and Nature spread before her in such innocent and happy charm, that savagery could haunt these lovely woodlands, and the shining river, or that the seemingly peaceful walls that surrounded her could harbor unjust and cruel men.

She turned from the window with a sigh; then remembering the solace that had come to her before she slept, she knelt again, and in her morning prayer there went up as earnest a cry for help and courage as ever left young lips. Then she clothed herself, thinking meanwhile of her who had with such signal opportuneness befriended her. Surely there would be many a service that she could perform that would attest her gratitude to Mistress Butler. Were it not for young Walter and his grandfather, how eagerly she might have hurried down the stair to her.

Nevertheless, Alison was not one to tarry when there were issues to be met. With a steady hand, and a brave heart, she undid the bar, and descended the stair.

Whereas in the evening she had seen the leaping fire filling the huge kitchen with ruddy cheer, now the sunshine poured its golden radiance through dozens of tiny glittering windowpanes, revealing the white freshness of the Dutch curtains, and the green and pink of the sturdy geraniums blooming on the wide sills. A striped blue and white linen pawn hung along the high mantel shelf. Pewter platters ranged their polished discs in the racks on the walls. A multitude of kitchen utensils hung there also, spotlessly clean, and ready for instant use, each one arranged in strictest order, for Maria Butler, coming from her Dutch home, had brought hither all those domestic arts and virtues, those habits of scrupulous neatness, for which her race is famed.

Maria herself, buxom and rosy-cheeked, wore her quilted petticoat short enough to show a pair of trim ankles, and gaily clocked stockings. Her blue and yellow bodice lay smooth over her ample bosom. Her morning cap of blue and yellow calico was set snug and close over her thick flaxen hair. Embodiment of a generous and capable housewife, the mere sight of her moving about her houseplace, brought a glow to the heart.

"A tidy woman, Roger would have called her," thought Alison, in wistful remembrance, coming through the kitchen door. Aloud she spoke a brave good morning.

"Ah, little one! Hast slept, I see," nodded Mistress Butler, approvingly, suspending her wooden ladle over a great pot of sputtering samp, that hung on a crane well above the blaze. "Art just in time to eat."

She dipped out liberally into a pair of porringers, and placed them steaming on the table drawn near to the hearth.

"We eat alone," she continued. "Colonel John made breakfast at sunrise, to get early back to

Fort Hunter. Walter ate with him, and now he is off to the stables, perhaps. Grandsir Butler takes always his morning meal in bed."

Relieved, as she knew the good-wife intended that she should be, that for a time at least she was to be free from unfriendly eyes, Alison sat down obediently in the seat assigned to her, took up the horn spoon beside her porringer, and willingly tasted of the hot samp flooded with yellow milk. She found it amazingly good, and made her meal in comfort, while Mistress Butler plied her with kindly questions.

"Thy father's chest came with thine own? Good! Pieter shall take it also to the room where thou hast slept. Thou wilt like to have it near thee, I know. It is sad that thou hast thy papers lost. Perhaps yet they will be found. Where was't that Walter set upon thee?"

"As I stood upon the public street before the tavern that has for its sign a black horse," replied Alison.

Maria's eyes grew round at this. "Shouldst never have been standing in such a place alone, child," she chided gently, shaking her close-capped head.

"Indeed, indeed, it is not my wont to do the like," pleaded Alison, and told her how it came about that she was there.

"Watson did ill to leave thee," declared Mistress Butler. "And Walter—he is a bold and forward lad. There has been too much sparing of the rod upon him. But, come, tell me now of what went before. How didst come to make this voyage?"

Then Alison told of her home in Kent, and all the story of her leaving it, and the sad end of what had been planned as a holiday adventure.

"Poor little one," sighed Mistress Butler, overflowing with sympathy. "So hard it has been for thee. But grieve not too much. In Maria Wemple thou hast a faithful friend who will do what she can to help thee."

"Maria Wemple!" protested a laughing voice behind her. "Darest still to call my Maria Butler by her girl name? Yet so it is—Maria Wemple, and Maria Wemple, and Maria Wemple— whenever we Butlers displease you. What's to do now, my sweeting?"

"Wat! My Wat!" exclaimed Maria, her blue eyes a-sparkle, and springing up in such haste that she came nigh to over-setting her half-emptied cup of tea. "'T is good to have thee home again! These four days thou'st been away, like four months have seemed!"

"And so to me," avowed her husband, for he

it was who had entered softly to take her by surprise. "Come, give me a kiss, my Maria Wemple, if so you must be called, and tell me of this new grievance, and who this strange maid may be." He turned smiling eyes upon Alison, who, Butler though she knew him, by a certain family look, yet found his countenance unmarred by that arrogance and cruelty that marked the others of his race.

"Then sit thee down to breakfast, Wat, and thou shalt hear," promised his wife, hasting to the hearth to fill bowl and cup for him, and to carve thick slices from the round of dried beef that stood upon the board. " 'T is Alison Blair, thy kin from England who sits here, and her story is no short one. Thou must be friend to her if thou wouldst please me."

"Friends, then, we are, Alison, since my good wife wills it, and here's my hand upon it. Forward with your tale, I beg of you."

Thus spoke Wat Butler, safe returned from his business in Schenectady, and while he ate heartily, and drank his tea cosily by the warm fireside, Alison vastly heartened that she had found this second ally, repeated yet again all that had befallen her in her journeyings.

Chapter x

WALTER BUTLER entered the open door of the barn.

A vast structure, roughly, yet strongly built, it was furnished below with capacious bins for the abundant harvests of grain, and roomy stalls for the horses and cattle. In the loft overhead, enormous mows overflowed with sweet-smelling hay.

The beasts had been turned out to pasture an hour ago, as he well knew, and Watson, so he believed, would be away in the fields. For this reason he had chosen this time and place, that he might be sure of being alone.

Silent though it was, and without sign of occupancy, he nevertheless took the precaution of going up and down every aisle, peering into every bin and stall, and at last of mounting the narrow ladder that led to the hayloft. Standing on its topmost round, he scanned the golden dusk. Except for a stray sunbeam or two, in which myriads of motes danced deliriously, it was apparently as untenanted as the floor below.

Thoroughly satisfied of his privacy, he climbed down again, and chose that one of the stalls farthest from the door in which, while keeping himself unseen, he was able at the same time to command a view of the doorway, so that none might enter the barn without his becoming instantly aware of it.

Until now, he had had no opportunity to examine unobserved a certain packet which he had filched from the pavement, and secreted in his wide coat sleeve, while he lay beaten and humiliated at the feet of his antagonist in the streets of New York, but he knew that it was Alison's for he had seen it fall, and he knew from its appearance that it contained something of consequence, so he had been content to wait for a safe occasion, such as he deemed the present one to be.

Leaning against the feed-rack, he slipped his hand into the bosom of his ruffled shirt, and drew out the packet. Bound securely to it by a narrow tape was the letter which Matthew Blair had sent to Captain Butler.

Walter plucked out the folded sheet, opened it, and read. Appeal though it was from one in the extremity of death, it aroused no faintest thrill of pity or compassion in his singularly cold-blooded nature.

"This fellow had a monstrous assurance," he sneered in an undertone, "when he sent his brat to settle down uninvited in my grandsir's house."

Refolding the sheet, he stuck it in the inner pocket of his coat, and proceeded to the examination of the packet. It was wrapped about with parchment, firmly tied, and marked with the name of Matthew Blair.

He undid the cord, unfolded the parchment, and turned over the contents with eager fingers.

Besides such personal documents as the journey made necessary for his daughter and himself, Dr. Blair had brought with him bank-notes to the amount of twelve hundred pounds, in clean one-hundred pound notes. Added to these were papers and memoranda relative to his properties in Kent, and to his monies in the Bank of England.

"Plenteous provision for the dear daughter, Alison," commented Walter mockingly, counting the notes one by one. "But this same sweet Alison shall have sterner experiences than her doting father thought, and under none too gentle tutors—myself among the number, in spite of my aunt, Mistress Butler."

He stood motionless, gloating over the bank-notes. It was the first time in his life that he had seen so large a sum of money, and the knowledge that he had power to revenge himself upon its rightful owner by withholding it from her, gratified him intensely.

As he thought upon it, a faint rustling, as of straw, overhead, arrested his attention. Although the sound ceased almost immediately, and might have had no other origin than that of mice playing about the mows, it was sufficient to put him on his guard. He slipped the packet quickly back into its cover, bound the letter upon it, and restored it to his breast. Then he stood waiting to see whether the sound would be repeated; but it was not.

Stealthily he crept to the ladder, and ascended it far enough to see into the loft. Standing there, with head bent, in an attitude of intent listening, was James Watson.

"How got you here, Watson?" demanded Walter brusquely, rising suddenly into full view.

Watson lifted his head with a jerk, and his face flamed red, but his answer was glib enough. "How got I here? Why, where should I be this time of morning, Master Butler, but about my work in the barn and thereabouts?"

Young Butler came the rest of the way, eyeing him suspiciously. "'T is but curiosity that makes me ask, Watson," he persisted, "because you were not here a few moments agone, and you have not passed threshold since."

"I guess you was a bit dazed by the sun, Master Butler, that you didn't see me whenst you was up afore. I seen you plain enough, myself," vowed Watson.

The man was plausible in his answer, but it did not escape Walter that as he spoke he made a covert movement with his foot as though to hide something beneath it. He was certain that unless Watson had been in concealment at the time that he had first inspected the loft he could not possibly have overlooked him. Yet why should he have concealed himself unless he wished to spy upon him? And if he had spied upon him, how had he accomplished it? He told himself that perhaps beneath the serving-man's foot, now held rigidly immovable, he might find the answer to his anxious questionings.

"For a man busy about his morning work,

James, you were prodigious still, and are so yet," he insinuated, as if in jest. "Are you glued to the loft floor in all this time, or have the witches got you? Nay, let me break their spell."

With a swift onrush, he threw himself upon him with all his weight, and Watson, taken altogether by surprise, staggered back, disclosing what his foot had until now successfully hidden. It was a fair-sized knot-hole in the flooring.

Walter stooped to it, and looked through. It furnished him a complete view of the stall below, the one in which he had been standing while he examined Matthew Blair's packet.

He sprang to his feet in a white fury.

"You dirty villain!" he flung at him, shaking his clenched fist. "You've been spying upon me!"

Watson faced his wrath doggedly. "Looks like spies was needed, maybe, Master Butler, from what I seen through that there hole. You're mighty proud of bein' a gentleman, descended from them Dukes of Ormonde, and yet you've as good as stole what belongs to a poor orphan lass, cousin to you and Captain. No better than a common thief, I calls it, to keep her father's papers, and her money from her. You're a mean one for certain, my young master! Wantin' to have her thrown out last night to them wild savages, as would scalp her in a minute, and this mornin' chucklin' over what you've got hid from her, and what'd keep her in her lady's place."

"What right have you to think that those papers belong to her?" thundered young Butler with flashing eyes.

"I'm most uncommon far-sighted, my master," asserted James Watson boldly, with arms akimbo. "Every word that you read standin' down there, I read from up here. Fortunit for the young lady that I did, say I, and your grandsir shall hear of it. That'll put her where she belongs, I guess."

Walter threw back his handsome head, and his scornful voice echoed through the dusky loft. "Go, by all means—by all means," he said, and there was menace in his eye. "Betray to my grandsir where these papers be, and I, on my side, will make known to him certain little transactions of yours, my honest Watson, at the Black Horse Tavern, concerning his beaverskins, and the like. If that be not enough, I can add to it an account of an interesting conversation overheard outside the fort-wall at Schenectady, which you held with Hooting Owl, the Caughnawaga."

His arrows shot, and quivering in the mark, young Butler gazed upon the would-be informant with coolest unconcern.

Watson's face mirrored his consternation, and for the moment he was dumb.

It was true that he had traded a bit of useful information concerning his countrymen, through Caughnawaga spies to the French, now and again, for the sake of valuable pelts to be gained thereby, and on occasion he had so managed his master's consignments of beaver-skins and flour to the New York factor, as to yield himself a neat profit, but all his dealings had been carefully planned for secrecy. Even if Walter had cleverly guessed at one or two of these transactions, or had overheard him, as he had hinted, upon these recent occasions, what actual proof had the lad that would be convincing to Captain Butler? None that he knew of.

He gathered himself together, determined to put up a bold front. " 'T is of no use going to your grandsir with such tales, Master Butler. I've served him well these many years, and never a penny out, as he very well knows. You'll not fright me with your boy's jokes from tellin' him what I seen in your hands this morning."

"Well and good," retorted Walter, unmoved.

"Cut your own throat, Watson. Here's proof enough against you." He drew from his vest pocket, with elaborate carelessness, a sheet of paper covered with dates and figures. "This memorandum of yours, dropped lately, will make my story clear."

Flirting it under the startled man's very nose, he restored it to his pocket before it could be snatched from him, and folded his arms above it. "Go, my good Watson. Go to my grandsir with your story, if you like."

Watson, instantly recognizing the paper for what young Butler claimed it to be, saw himself ensnared. With dropped jaw, he stood momentarily irresolute, and then took a desperate resolve. Like a flash he leapt at the taunting figure, with his powerful arms outstretched grimly.

"You'll just give up that bit o' paper, my young master, or we'll see who's who," he asserted between set teeth.

But Walter was too quick for him. Lithe as a tiger cat, he sprang backward, and as he sprang he snatched a pistol from his breast pocket and cocked it. His voice rang icy clear. "You may have forgotten it, James, but I'm a dead shot. One step farther and I fire."

Watson, with the weapon covering him, felt

the cold sweat bedew his forehead. He knew
that the finger on the trigger was steady, and
that the aim would be sure. Had he not, times
without number, seen bird, deer, and fox fall
before that unerring marksman? Well, luck was
against him, and he must make the best of a bad
matter that he could. A sickly smile overspread
his shrewd features.

"Have't as you like, Master Butler," he
conceded sullenly. "Since you and me's both a
bit off the honest, I'll take you up on your bargain. I'll keep a quiet tongue, and so'll you."

One last fling he could not resist, however,
and his tone was defiant as he gave it: "But mark
you, now, my young sir! If ever you plays me
false, I'll go to more than your gran'sir about
that packet behind your shirt ruffles, cost me
what it will, and that I warn you."

And with this Watson left him.

The question of how soon he should be able
to secrete Alison's packet elsewhere than on his
own person, gave Walter far more solicitude
than did Watson's threat. He knew quite well
that he dared not use any of the bank-notes
for a very long time to come, for none of them
being of lower value than one hundred pounds
apiece, he could not, circumstanced as he was,

have a single one of them exchanged without exciting suspicion and inquiry. If, however, he could lodge them in some safe spot, he would eventually be able to do with them as he pleased. The papers it would be easy enough to destroy, but this, for the present at least, he did not wish to do. It would yield him a far keener satisfaction to know that they were still in existence, yet withheld from Alison.

He could not take them with him to Fort Hunter, where a large family of inquisitive young brothers and sisters made secrecy in regard to any matter both difficult, and uncertain. No, he would hide them where they would be in actual reach of Alison, and yet so guarded from her that there would be no possible risk of their discovery. He remembered just such a place.

Leaving the dim quiet of the barn, he passed slowly out into the sunshine, and on toward the house, whipping the heads from the flowers along his path with a slender switch snatched from a birch tree. It was as though he must ever be striking at the defenceless things, and the weak.

A sound of voices in the stone spring-house told him that Mistress Butler, and her negro slave, Calista, were within, skimming the cream from the shallow bowls of milk that had been cooling in the little stream that ran along in a wooden trough set in the brick floor. A word or two that he caught informed him that they would be absent from the house for some time. Captain Butler, at this hour, was usually still in bed, having laid aside, on passing his eightieth year, the habit of early rising.

There would be none, therefore, whom he might expect to encounter except Alison, herself. She would be in the kitchen, perhaps, put to some household task by Mistress Butler. In that case the occasion for hiding the packet would not yet be ripe, but he might console himself for that by tormenting her in some fashion. At this alluring prospect he quickened his pace.

The kitchen had a divided door. The upper half of it was open, affording a view of the interior of the room. No one was there. The brisk ticking of the moon-faced clock, and the purring of a green stick on the andirons only served to make the stillness more intense. Walter raised the massive iron latch of the lower section of the door, and entered on tiptoe. Looking into buttery, hall, and dining-room, he found them untenanted also. The door of Captain Butler's sleeping chamber was fast closed.

In the parlor the old man's armchair stood vacant before a dying fire; his slippers were warming upon the wide brick hearth. The sunbeams that touched the hunting-prints on the walls, and struck rich splashes of prismatic color from a multitude of crystal drops ornamenting the candelabra upon the low mantel-shelf, were the only living things in the silent room.

He paused on the threshold, listening, but not a human creature was stirring in the house. His opportunity had come sooner than he had dared to hope, and he immediately embraced it. Entering the parlor, he closed the door softly behind him. If Alison, who had seen him approaching while he was yet at some distance from the house, and had retired in precipitate haste to her little room under the eaves, could have known what he was about to do behind that shut door, she would have descended unhesitatingly, and confronted him boldly, demanding her property, but in her ignorance she remained sequestered, the protecting bar across her door, congratulating herself that she was out of reach of his persecutions.

Walter went straight to the chimney-piece.

On either side of the enormous fireplace were narrow paneled cupboards. He opened the door of one at the right. The wall within was rough and unfinished, showing the unplastered bricks behind the shelves. Ranged decorously upon the shelves were a multitude of articles in daily use: a sheaf of goose-quills for penmaking, a half dozen candles, a tinder-box, Captain Butler's flask and horn drinking-cup, his canister of best imported snuff, a jar of tobacco, an ivory sheath for Maria's knitting needles.

Inserting his hand delicately above the objects on the midmost shelf, Walter took pains to disarrange none of them. He pressed upon a brick, distinguished a trifle from the rest by a slight unevenness of surface. It gave a little under his fingers, although to the eye it appeared as firmly fixed as its fellows. In a moment he had lifted it out, and disclosed a hollow between the space that it had occupied and the masonry behind it. It was a hiding-place that he had used more than once before.

He made haste to see whether it would contain the packet. It was none too large, yet it received it, and when the brick was replaced, no one could have guessed that Alison's treasure was concealed behind it.

Chapter xi

FORTUNE had favored Walter by but a narrow margin, for he had not yet withdrawn his hand from the cupboard when the door of the parlor was pushed open, and a voice spoke him jovially:

"How now, young Walter? What is't that you are seeking there, among your grandsir's snuff-cans and flasks?"

Walter, a long gray goose-quill in his supple fingers, turned a blandly smiling face to the speaker. "I seek nothing more harmful to my years than a quill, good Uncle Wat. My pen is grievously worn out," and so saying, he closed the cupboard door.

"Let quills be, Walter, in this sweet spring weather, and go a-hunting instead," said Lieutenant Butler, taking down his own rifle from the rack above the chimney, and handing a second to his nephew. "Your aunt will not take amiss a bit of game for the spit, I'll warrant."

Alison, from her room overhead, presently

saw the two emerge into the open, with game bags slung across their shoulders. They strode with elastic steps across the springing grass, over the cleared fields, and so off into the forest.

Assured by this that she need have no fear of their return for some hours at least, she went down to the kitchen, where Mistress Butler was now engaged with her usual household tasks. Alison was soon given a place in her activities. She slipped into it gently and unobtrusively, helping to press out the warmed curd for the making of cheese, learning to cut neat lumps of sugar for the silver bowl, from the tall sugar cone, grinding spices at the mill for the pudding to be eaten at dinner. Calista, busy with the rough chores and heavier work, sang in an undertone a negro melody of such strangely haunting and curious charm that Alison kept one ear bent to it, while with the other she hearkened to the cheerful flow of conversation with which Mistress Butler enlivened their joint labors.

In this fashion the morning slipped pleasantly away, and the dinner-hour arrived, bringing back the hunters, hungry and laden with game. Whatever had been said to Walter by his uncle during their absence, it had given him to know that Alison was not to be the subject of annoyance or persecution by him. And so, in the presence of the Lieutenant and his wife he contented himself by showing her a mock courtesy that deceived his elders, although Alison herself could clearly perceive the sneer beneath it. Captain Butler, to her relief, ignored her altogether, and so her first meal in his company proved less hard to bear than she had supposed it possibly could be.

When dinner was done, and she was left alone again with Mistress Butler, she had her first lesson in spinning. Industry was natural to Alison. To all that she did, moreover, she brought a quickness of instinct, and a graceful dexterity of hand that recommended her more and more to her teacher.

"Thou has the right touch, little one," said Maria Butler approvingly, as she superintended the moistening of the flax by her pupil, and the twisting of the filament, while by the movement of the wheel it was wound upon the bobbins. "Of thee I shall soon make a good spinner."

The words and tone warmed Alison's lonely heart, and she redoubled her efforts to learn, and to be of use. Given an assured and sheltered place under the wing of this kindly soul, she felt that she could support undismayed whatever she might have to endure at the hands of Captain Butler or his grandson.

"Yes, yes, thou wilt make a good spinner," repeated Maria Butler, when all the bobbins were filled, and they began to wind the thread in knots and skeins upon the reel, "and a good daughter thou wouldst be in any house. I could wish to keep thee always with me."

To this Alison made no reply, except to reel the faster.

But if the housewife was pleased with the aptness of her pupil in learning to spin, she was all the more delighted to find that she was already a skilful knitter, for many a pair of fine black silken hose had Alison made in England for her father.

That evening, while the family sat, as was their wont, in the parlor, Captain Butler at backgammon with his grandson, Lieutenant Wat turning over the leaves of *The Gentleman's Magazine* borrowed from a friend and neighbor —Colonel William Johnson, Mistress Butler, erect and smiling in the tapestried chair, plying her needle industriously, Alison took a candle and went to get from her traveling chest her own knitting-needles to set up a pair of ornamental hose for her benefactress.

She was glad enough to absent herself for at least a few moments from the supercilious glances shot at her covertly by Walter in the pauses of his game.

She had not yet returned when a sharp rat-tat of the iron knocker upon the front door of the house brought Wat Butler to his feet.

"It has the sound of Will Johnson," he said to his wife in passing. "Yet it can scarce be that he is so soon home from the Governors' meeting in Virginia."

William Johnson it was, though, as he saw when the light of the opening door streamed out over the figure beyond the threshold.

Wat grasped his hand, and drew him in to the firelight and candlelight, crying, "A welcome to you, Will. We had not thought to see you in another sennight."

"Faith, nor I you, Wat," replied the newcomer, bowing over Maria's plump fingers, and shaking the Captain and Walter heartily by the hand, "but I'd better luck in the whole of it than I look for at all."

While the newcomer dropped off his full

cloak, and laid aside his laced beaver, Captain Butler had shoved back the board and pieces, saying abruptly to his grandson, "No more of this, Walter." Then to William Johnson, with a cordiality that he showed to few: "Come, Will, and sit. Let's have your news about the campaign. We're all athirst for it."

"'T was victory for me all round," began Johnson, with a note of elation in his voice, dropping into the chair that Wat had placed for him. "There were Governors from five states at the Council: old Dinwiddie of Virginia, crabbed, but not so bad as his bark; Morris from Quaker Pennsylvania; Sharpe from Maryland; our own Delancey; and Shirley from Massachusetts, shrewd, and on the lookout for his own state, but favoring me from the start, and winning General Braddock to the same way of thinking. 'T was first, that I should have full power to treat with the Five Nations, and next, the commission of sole Superintendent of Indian Affairs."

"None so fit as yourself for that," interposed Wat Butler heartily. "We all know, Will, that the Iroquois love and trust you full as much as they hate the traders in Albany, who've cheated 'em, and abused 'em, ever since they took charge of their affairs when you threw up the job in disgust in 1748, after Aix la Chapelle."

"True it is that I can do more with 'em than any other man," agreed Johnson, with pardonable pride, "but then haven't I always been fair to 'em, and let them in and out of my house as if they were my own brothers. The doorstep and the halls of Mount Johnson are cluttered with 'em, by day and by night."

"Yes, you've always kept the Iroquois solid for us," commended Captain Butler. "But go on, Will, I can see you've more to tell us."

"Well, to make a long tale short, Captain, they've commissioned me a major-general, and put me in command to lead an expedition against Crown Point, as soon as we can get our troops gathered from the Provinces that have promised to join in the campaign."

There was a little buzz of congratulation as Johnson gave this out that pleased him mightily, for he did not lack an ample share of vanity and self-consequence. His pride was not without genuine foundation, however, for his remarkable influence over the Indian Confederacy, won by years of just treatment and generosity toward its members, has never been equalled or approached by any other. He had given them sympathy and understanding, he had settled their difficulties to their satisfaction, and fed their widows and orphan children in time of famine and distress. Familiar with their tribal customs, speaking their language fluently, he went in and out among them as freely as though he were of Indian blood.

He was about to go on with his account of the doings of the Council at Alexandria, when a faint rustle in the doorway caught his quick ear. Turning, he saw Alison, a slender, sweet-faced maid, pausing irresolute on the threshold, uncertain whether or not to enter, now that this guest was among them, and with business perhaps of a private nature.

At sight of her, he sprang to his feet, his face as white as paper, his hands pressed convulsively to his heart.

"Alison!" he gasped, and again, "Alison! My God! How come you here?" Transfixed and staring, he waited for her answer, his tongue dried in his mouth.

Astounded at hearing herself addressed thus by a total stranger, Alison stared back at him speechless.

In that strong face, with its high and commanding forehead, its grave and arching brows, its large thin-lipped mouth, great nose, and un-flinching chin, she discerned no likeness to any-one that she had ever known.

The General brushed his hand heavily across his eyes, as though to clear his vision; yet when he looked again, he saw as before the slight fig-ure of a girl, with large eyes of clearest gray, soft clustering locks of chestnut brown, cheeks flushing and paling under the intentness of his gaze.

Those who looked on were no less amazed than Alison at this strange outburst of emo-tion. How could they guess, any more than she, that William Johnson beheld in her the exact counterpart of a sweet Irish maid, whom he had deeply loved in early youth, but had been for-bid to win. Buried in his heart, beneath the dust of years, she was still a cherished memory. He had little deemed that her living, breathing im-age could rise up thus before him in this wilder-ness of the New World.

But common sense awoke ere long, and told him that this could not be the Alison whom he had known, for youth does not tarry through the years, even in the loveliest and most dear. Yet, though this maid could not be she, must she not be of her blood?

By a visible effort he pulled himself together. "Who is it that you are?" he stammered.

The girl found voice. "I am Alison," she replied simply—"Alison Blair."

"Your mother?" he asked it quickly.

"Alison Doane."

"Of County Clare?" continued he, his eyes still eagerly searching her face.

"Yes," breathed she, surprised beyond measure at this unlooked-for knowledge in a stranger.

"Your father?"

"Dr. Matthew Blair, of Kent," she said, and her voice soared sweetly, for love and pride of him whom she had so lately lost.

"It is the same," murmured General Johnson in a monotone.

To Mistress Butler, as to one who could understand, he turned, with a sigh, and a mournful smile upon his lips. "Once I knew the mother of her," he said. "Sweet lass she was, as ever drew breath of Irish air."

"So did my father always say," cried Alison softly, her face aglow.

"And this lass is her mother's self," mused Johnson, half aloud. "But what's brought the tender child to this wild land?"

"She comes to me claiming shelter on the

score of distant kinship, with a tale of parents dead, papers lost, and the like," Captain Butler informed him acidly, with a contemptuous glance at the young girl standing poised in the doorway.

General Johnson wheeled to him. " 'T is the lucky man you are, Captain Butler, to have a lass like this come to your door, whatever brings her," and he went to Alison and drew her in, handing her to a seat as though she were a queen.

"It's an honor I would fain be without," snapped the old man. Unwelcome discovery this was to him, indeed, that William Johnson should have found in this creature the daughter of an early love, and could be moved by her in such fashion. It would mean no less than that he himself would be forced to acknowledge her, and treat her with at least some show of decency and consideration, however grudging.

Nor did young Walter like the thought that here was sprung up a powerful friend and ally for Alison where none could have expected it. It would make more difficult, more necessary to veil with perfect secrecy, his planting of thorns along her way.

As for Wat, he smiled kindly upon the girl,

where she sat, with bent head, trying with trembling fingers to set the stitches upon her needles.

Mistress Butler spoke her feeling openly. "You have right, William Johnson. She should find welcome. With me, and with my husband she has it, and kindness she shall receive from us both."

"Well, well," growled Captain Butler, testily, "let's have an end of this maid's affairs. With the matter of Crown Point and Ticonderoga forward, we've things of greater import to spend our time upon."

So the talk turned again to the Council at Alexandria, and the plans that had been made there, but every now and then, even in the midst of some weighty sentence, the General's glance wandered to Alison sitting in the shadow, and rested upon her with a brooding tenderness softening the eagle keenness of his eyes.

At last he rose. "I've great need now of a clever lad of a white man," he said, "to help out Captain Peter Wraxall with all the secretary work he'll be doing. I've writ to Ross to look out for one for me, but 't will be slow work finding a man to my heart."

In the act of donning his cloak, the General chanced to look at Walter, and caught upon the boy's face a fleeting expression, vanishing quickly, but profoundly sinister. It had been directed at the unconscious Alison.

Instantly, as though he had but that moment remembered something that he had meant to speak of sooner, General Johnson addressed him: "You'll be riding to Mount Johnson with me tonight, Walter, I hope, to surprise my boy John. He's that wearied of his own company, and he'll take it ill if you go back to Fort Hunter without giving him a bit of your time. You can go pillion behind me, and not trouble to take out a horse."

An invitation from General Johnson was not to be lightly refused, and Walter, sweet as was the prospect of being able to annoy Alison in a hundred surreptitious ways should he remain where he was, did not hesitate to accept, for he and young John Johnson had been boon companions from infancy, and Mount Johnson, with its manifold interests and activities, and its opportunities for untrammeled freedom, with hosts of Indians, and men of the woods incessantly coming and going, held out attractions that he never could resist. He hastened away, therefore, to make ready.

General Johnson's final words were for Alison. "Remember, my lass," he told her gravely, taking her hand in a powerful grasp, "you've only to come to me, when there's anything I can be doing for you. You'll find the door to my heart always wide open to your sweet mother's daughter." With that, he stooped from his great height, and touched her forehead gently with his lips.

Chapter xii

MISTRESS MARIA, butter-making in the dairy-house, sang the time-honored churning-song of the Dutch:

"Buitterchee, buitterchee, comm;
Alican, laidlechee, tubichee voll."

Calista, her dusky wool bound down by a gorgeous-hued bandana of scarlet and yellow and green cotton cloth, her stiffly starched purple calico dress rattling with every movement of her body, poured the skim milk into buckets for the pigs, and scoured the milk pans.

A little brook, fed by a spring higher up the hill, ran through the dairy in a flat trough, built deep and wide to hold in icy coolness the great crocks of milk and cream and butter.

Its duty done, the crystal water escaped beyond the walls, and spread itself gaily out into shallows between grassy banks, and gurgling happily for a while under the open sky, sped on into the shadowy forest, there to leap and swirl and rush over pebbly sun-dappled reaches, and down

rocky slopes, mingling at last with the broad
sweep of the Mohawk.

A few yards below the dairy the water-cresses
grew thick, and Alison, a flat willow-basket in
her hand, gathered them for the noon-day salad.
Shaking the bright water-drops from each green
stalk before she laid it in the basket, she hum-
med the butter-song in unison with Mistress
Maria.

All at once the voice at the churn was abruptly
stilled. The song-charm had worked, and the
butter was come. Soon Alison heard the spat,
spat, of the butter-paddles, pressing the milk
from the yellow mass.

Before long the clatter of horse's hoofs broke
in upon this homely pleasant sound. It was General Johnson, astride his roan mare, rising and
falling in his saddle, English fashion, as he
trotted up the hill road to the house.

Mistress Butler saw him through the open
door. She laid down her paddles, and made
straight her spotless linen cap, gone half an
inch awry.

"Kleintje," she called to Alison, "General
Johnson comes, I go to see if he stays to dinner.
Finish me the working of this butter, please. Thy
hand will be so good as mine."

Proud to be trusted, eagerly hoping that General Johnson would be persuaded to remain, Alison came at once, set down her basket, rolled back her sleeves, and took up the paddles.

"Ah," nodded Mistress Butler approvingly, eyeing the cresses, "thou hast picked fine ones. Those go well with the dinner. Bring them, Calista. And, Alison, forget not to make fast the dairy when thou hast finished."

She laid a huge key upon the table, and bustled away, the negro wench following, with the overflowing basket poised upon her head.

Alison, left alone in the dairy, pressed the soft mass of butter deftly into hardness and shape. She had watched Mistress Butler at the work more than once, and knew how it should be done. She was fond of the dairy. The cool, clean, brick floor, the rough stone walls, the trickling of the water through the trough, the glittering pans and shining crocks and their contents appealed to her housekeeping sense.

When the butter lay firm and freed from every drop of moisture, she lifted it out of the wooden bowl into a crock, packed it down, covered it, and set it in the running stream.

She was pouring the buttermilk from the churn, when all at once there was a blotting of the light from the door. A swift glance in that direction showed her so wild a figure standing between her and any avenue of escape, that she was filled with terror, but in an instant she saw that though it was human creature, it was no savage, but a youth in torn garments, with matted overhanging hair, that half hid his face. He tottered toward her as one at the end of his strength, and now she saw him more clearly.

"You!" she cried, and started forward, peering at him in amazement. In spite of haggard looks, and sunken eyes, of raiment worn to tatters, and shaggy locks, she recognized in him the one who had come gallantly to her aid before the Black Horse Tavern.

"You," he echoed faintly, sinking exhausted upon the damp brick floor at her feet. For an instant Alison knew not what to do, but his lean and famished appearance made her certain that he stood in sore need of food. She snatched up a dipper and filled it with cool sweet milk. Kneeling beside him, she put it to his lips.

"Drink," she urged.

With the eagerness of one who has fasted long, he put a shaking hand to the draught, and pressed it closer.

"What brings you here in this sad state?"

asked Alison pitifully, when the dipper was drained.

"The savages," he gasped. "They took me captive where I hunted with my uncle. I have escaped from them, but they pursue me. Oh, do not let them take me!" His voice died away, but his eyes, in anguished appeal, held hers. Pinched nostrils and drawn cheeks showed how spent he was.

"Where are they?" demanded Alison.

He rallied himself. "On the river," he replied, so low that she barely heard. "They are searching the shore. They will find the brook, and guess that I have followed it, that I might leave no trail. At any moment they may be here."

Alison stepped quickly to a tiny window in the dairy-wall opposite to the door. It faced the forest. She pushed open its wooden shutter, and looked out, but saw no one.

That did not reassure her. She had heard only too often how stealthily the Indian approaches to fall upon his victim at unawares. Peaceful and untenanted as the forest seemed to be, innocently as the brook chattered away into its shade, who could be sure that even the nearest tree-trunks did not shelter dusky forms with hands on knives or tomahawks, or that at this instant, filing silently up the bed of the brook on moccasined feet, there might not be the fierce pursuers of this boy who crouched trembling upon the dairy floor.

Swiftly she drew in the heavy shutter, and barred it. Upon the table, where Mistress Butler had left it, lay the key to the dairy-house door. She caught it up.

"Stay you here," she said, "and make no sound. The savages shall not recapture you. I dare not take you from this shelter, lest they should be near, but locked in the dairy-house you will be safe until I can bring help."

There was confidence in her voice, for had not General Johnson, all powerful with the Indians, come as by God's mercy, but a few moments since. It was to him that she could go, and find assured succor.

The dark misery upon the boy's face lifted at her words, but before he could answer, she was gone, the door fast shut behind her, the ponderous key turned in the lock.

Gathering up her skirts that she might run the faster, Alison dashed up the narrow path to the house. General Johnson she might expect to find seated in the parlor. A black frown would undoubtedly be given her by Captain Butler for

daring to break in upon them while they talked
over, as they often did, important Indian matters. But with this poor lad in such extreme
peril, she would care nothing for that.

To her dismay, when she had but half covered the distance, she heard the shoes of Queen
Bess striking on the gravel of the driveway.
That meant that General Johnson had not
stayed—that she might not be able to catch him
before he was out of her reach.

Hoping to intercept him, she changed her
direction, and sped down the slope, breaking
through bushes and low shrubs, in her impetu-
ous haste, and as she went, she cried aloud,
"General Johnson! General Johnson!"

Queen Bess was quickening into a trot when
Alison darted out upon the road, scarce a yard
behind her. General Johnson, turning in the
saddle, waved his beaver to her without drawing
rein.

"Stop, stop!" she shrilled, her voice rising
high above the clatter of the horse's hoofs. "Oh
stop! There's life and death at stake!"

William Johnson brought his mare to an
abrupt stand. "What mean you, Alison?" he
demanded.

"A lad," she panted, at his side now, "who

once befriended me, is yonder in the dairy, hiding from savages! You have such power. Oh, come, come, and rescue him."

"Never tremble so, my lass," said the General reassuringly. "They shan't harm a hair of him." He lowered himself from the saddle, and tied Queen Bess to the nearest tree. The mare, disappointed of a speedy return to her noon-day stabling, tossed her mane with an impatient whinny.

Knowing well how important it was that the Indians should not reach the fugitive first, William Johnson moved with rapid strides across the slope.

"How came the lad to fall among savages?" he inquired of Alison, as she ran to keep up with him.

"He was hunting with his uncle when a band of Mohawks captured him," she replied.

"Captured him?" repeated Johnson, stopping short.

"Yes," returned Alison. "But, oh, come quickly, General Johnson."

" 'T is a different matter, my girl, if he was captive to the Mohawks," he told her shaking his head. "I cannot help him in such a case."

"You cannot help him!" she cried astounded, catching at his arm. "Oh, what can you mean?"

"This," returned he: "Indian never interferes with Indian in the matter of captives."

"But you are no Indian," she declared.

"I have been made a blood brother to the Mohawks," he explained, "and since these be Mohawks I must let him go. If they did but pursue him, it would be easy to save him had I but caught him first. As it is——" he shrugged his shoulders to show that what she asked was impossible to grant.

"Surely you cannot mean what you say, sir. It is not Christian!" protested Alison piteously. "He is in sore distress and danger. You cannot give him over to torture and death, or, at the best, captivity."

"It is the law of the savage, and I have sworn to them to respect it," declared Johnson. "Yet, 't is sorry enough I am to refuse you, lass."

Alison pressed her hands to her breast to hold back a sob. Her great eyes pierced him with her agonized pleading. "You said you were my mother's friend, when you were a lad, like this one yonder," she breathed. "Save him, then, for her sake, for she was gentle, and tender of heart, and could not have seen him delivered over to savages."

"It's a hard thing you're wanting of me, Alison. Your mother, oh—I loved her well, when I was a lad, and 't is gall to me to refuse what you're asking in the name of her, but I'd lose all power with the Mohawks if I didn't keep faith with them." He paused, irresolute, eyes fixed on the ground, and the girl, anxiously watching his face, saw written there the struggle between his desire to grant her plea, and his determination to keep faith with Indian custom.

She saw the look of yielding pass, and give place to one of settled grimness.

"They'd not give him, if I should ask 'em," he asserted, and swung slowly about as though to go to his horse.

Alison took a desperate resolve. "Since you will do naught for him," she said, and her voice rang sharply, and her eyes flashed stern, "go back, General Johnson, and I will go to him alone. You are no friend to my mother, nor to me."

"You shall not go, Alison," declared Johnson, turning quickly, to catch her by the wrists. " 'T would be death for you, or worse."

"Then let it be so." and now her voice broke.

"He stood my friend, when I was defenceless and alone, as he is now. He waits for me in hope, and I will not forsake him." She tore herself free, and ran, as if for dear life, to the diary-house.

Johnson, with a swift glance toward the forest, detected no sign that the Mohawks had as yet discovered the trail of the fugitive. Muttering under his breath, he strode after the determined girl, and reached her as she turned the key in the lock. He made no attempt to check her.

She darted him a look of inquiry.

"Alison," he whispered, and she saw the keenness of his brown eyes melt, "I'll do what I can to save the lad, for your mother's sake, but I may try in vain."

Without a word, Alison bent and brushed his hand with her cheek. Then she pushed open the door, and they went in together.

Chapter xiii

THE lad, crouching in the farthest corner of the dairy, rose to his feet at the sound of the opening door. While he had been waiting for Alison's return he had won back his courage.

General Johnson scanning him swiftly from head to foot, knew him at once for a manly, intelligent fellow, through all disguise of wretched garments, dust of the way, and the miseries that an Indian's captive is forced to endure. His warm heart went out to him. His shrewd head saw how it might be possible to rescue him.

"Your name, my lad?" he demanded, without preface.

"Mark Renshaw, sir," the boy answered promptly, brushing back the tangled hair that overhung his brow like a thatch.

"Whence come you?" went on the General briskly.

"From the city of New York," returned Mark.

"You were made captive by Mohawks while you hunted?"

"Yes, sir."

"Your uncle—what befel him?"

"The knife of the savage, sir." The lad's face blanched at the memory, but he held himself steady.

"A Mohawk shows scant mercy," commented the General briefly. "You have been schooled?" he went on.

"Yes, sir."

"You write a fair hand, and cipher well?"

Astonished that the General should ask such questions, while life only seemed the issue of the hour, Alison listened tensely.

Surprise showed in the countenance of Mark, also, but he gave his replies as though they and the questions themselves were all that mattered.

"My uncle thought to have me with him in his business when I was of proper age," he said, "and so I write well, and have been trained to figures."

"Your parents—where are they?"

"Dead, sir, since I was but a mere babe."

"Your aunt?"

" 'T is but a half-aunt, sir, and a hard woman. She has never been friend to me. Like enough she is glad to have me gone." There was a trace of bitterness in his tone.

A sound, so faint that even Alison's sharp ears did not detect it, came perceptibly to the forest-trained hearing of General Johnson. He spoke more rapidly:

"The Mohawks are here. Take yourself to the farther wall, Alison, and speak not a single word, if you would have this matter go well. Mark, stand you here, behind me, and for your life's sake neither stir, nor utter one syllable. I'll do all in my power to save you, but I'll answer for nothing if you disobey me."

The last word had scarcely passed his lips when a tall Mohawk appeared just outside the dairy-house. He was naked, save for a loin cloth, and from his scalp lock rose a single eagle feather. At one sweep his glittering eyes took in the occupants of the little enclosure, yet, surprised though he must have been to find General Johnson confronting him there, he manifested no faintest sign of it. His ferocious and warlike countenance was wooden. Straight as an arrow, he advanced to the threshold, and following close after him, their features as rigidly immobile as his own, their copper-hued bodies clad as scantily, came six of his fellow-warriors.

Alison noted with horror that none lacked his girdle of dangling scalps; saw, too, the glistening knives, and tomahawks that each one wore.

General Johnson spoke first:

"Welcome, Red Fox," he said.

"Ugh," grunted Red Fox, and folding his arms, remained stationary in the doorway.

"Have not my brothers wandered from their trail?" smiled Johnson, lessening the distance between himself and the chieftain by a foot. "Welcome are my brothers, and at Mount Johnson my door stands ever open to the coming of their feet; but I looked not for you before the moon was round, nor until your wigwams had first been made glad by your return. Do not the squaws and old men at Canajoharie Castle wait to hear of your deeds upon the war-path, and to count the scalps upon your belts?"

"Red Fox returns not to his lodge without his captive," answered the savage. "How would the old men and the squaws laugh and point scornfully at him, if he brings no captive for the torture, and to give sport to the village!" His glance shot significantly beyond William Johnson to where Mark stood motionless, his eyes fixedly regarding the brick floor.

"Never can squaws or old men point scornful

fingers at my brother, Red Fox," declared Johnson, drawing yet nearer to the Indian. "Instead,
they will sing his praises when he tells them the
story of these scalps, and how they were taken."

"There is no need that Red Fox should come
to the village with shame because he has no captive," replied the chieftain, a crafty smile breaking for the first time the fixed expression of his
countenance, "for has not my brother, William
Johnson, caught him when he escaped from Red
Fox, and has he not kept him for him until he
could overtake him?"

"Swift are the feet of Red Fox, and his scent
is keen on the trail," returned Johnson. "No captive fleet enough to escape him, or cunning
enough to hide his trail from the great chief's
eyes or those of his brother warriors, has come
this way."

"Let not my brother say so," and Red Fox, as
he spoke, fixed the General with a piercing gaze.
"Is not my captive behind him? My brother has
only to give him to me, and the Mohawks will
take him at once, and carry him away to their
village." With his right arm extended toward
Mark, and the other crossed upon his breast, he
waited as one who does not expect his demand
to be refused.

Alison, listening, trembled for the General's answer, and Mark became more deathly white of cheek, but both kept a silence as of death.

General Johnson returned the gaze of the savage with well feigned astonishment.

"Surely, this cannot be the lost captive of the great chief. Not in a hundred winters of the smoke of the lodge fires would the eyes of Red Fox grow so dull on the trail, nor his feet so slow that he could be left behind by this weak and miserable boy."

The Indian flushed. "The swiftest warrior runs not while he sleeps at night, and in the morning the river and the creek have left no trail that he can follow," he said haughtily.

William Johnson changed his tone. "If, then, this is your captive, he must go with you," he said, and paused.

Mark's form grew rigid, but beyond that he gave no sign. Alison, remembering barely in time the warning that had been given her, pressed her hand hard over her mouth to still the cry of protest that rose to her lips.

Red Fox crossed the sill. His companions drew to the doorway.

General Johnson raised a restraining hand. "Wait but a moment, my brothers," he said, and

his words came evenly, and almost with indifference, as though he were proposing no great
matter. "This is the captive of Red Fox, for so he
has told me, and to his brother he will not lie.
But is it not true that so brave a warrior as he
may return with scalps instead of captives and
meet no scorn? Or may he not sell his captives,
if he wishes, especially so miserable a one as this,
when his brother asks it, and is willing to pay
his price? For many moons has William Johnson sought for a youth to write in his books, and
mark in them the number of his beaver-skins,
and the bushels of corn that he keeps ready for
the widowed squaws and orphaned children in
winter when they are hungry, and the white
mantle of snow covers the bare fields. He has
sent many times to seek a youth to help Captain
Peter Wraxall in his work for your brother, but
none whom he can trust has come. Will not my
brother, Red Fox, sell this captive to me, to help
me in my need?"

From behind him Johnson heard Mark stir
ever so slightly.

The brows of Red Fox drew together while
he considered the proposal. It was true, as his
white brother had said: his fame would not be
tarnished if he chose to come to his lodge with-

General Johnson raised a restraining hand,
"Wait but a moment, my brothers."

out captives, provided he did not come without scalps. Moreover, the boy was already too weak and exhausted by hardships to provide long sport for the village.

General Johnson waited, his mien impassive, as is expected of the blood-brother of an Indian, when a bargain is proposed, or a council is in progress.

After some moments of silent calculation, Red Fox spoke: "What will my brother give?" There was a flicker of cupidity in the veiled coldness of his beady eyes.

"A loin-cloth," answered Johnson, as though the captive were of no greater value.

Red Fox shook his head. "If my brother has hunted for many moons for one to help him in his work, he should be willing to pay more. Let Red Fox take his captive, and go."

General Johnson heard Mark breathe short, and though he knew that an Indian cannot be hurried in a bargain, he could not find it in his heart to keep the lad longer in suspense. "What will Red Fox take, then, for his captive?" he inquired, maintaining his assumed indifference.

"Let my brother give me two blankets, a knife, and a roll of bright calico, and it will be enough," returned the Indian.

"The price of Red Fox is high, but if he will go at once to Mount Johnson, it shall be paid him," was the answer, "but let him not forget that I have bought the youth, and he is mine." There was warning in the General's tone, and in his level gaze.

Red Fox bowed. "My brother has spoken," he said. "Red Fox has given his word, and the word of a Mohawk to his brother Mohawk is not the word of a lying Algonquin."

In another moment he was gone, and with him his companions, but not before General Johnson had spoken a few words to them in Mohawk, to which they had replied gravely in the same tongue. By the gesture of William Johnson's hand in her direction and by the intentness with which the savages had regarded her, Alison guessed that his words had concerned herself as well as Mark.

As soon as the redskins had departed, the General turned. For Mark's stammered gratitude he had a genial laugh, and the hearty reply: "Nay, not so fast with your thanks, my lad. By the time Peter Wraxall has kept you quill-driving for a week, you may think you've not tumbled head first into a down-bed at all."

To what Alison whispered into his bent ear, he returned, his eyes a-twinkle:

"Sure, what else could I be doing, darlin'? There's Mohawks and Mohawks, and with you threatening to throw yourself to the savages, I thought you'd be safer with the counterfeit than with the real article. Now run off with you to Mistress Butler, and tell her I'll be staying to dinner after all. This lad here'll be the better for a meal first, and some whole clothes on his back, before I take him up behind me on Queen Bess to Mount Johnson."

For the second time that morning, Alison raced at top speed toward the house on the hill. A scant half-hour had there been between, but for Mark it had measured the distance between captivity and freedom, and for Alison terrified suspense and the power to proclaim a fortunate deliverance.

Chapter xiv

CANTERING along the highroad on Queen Bess with Mark behind him, General Johnson learned the details of the lad's capture and escape. Hunting in the forest, in the neighborhood of New York, with his uncle and a party of friends, they had been surprised by Red Fox and his band. All but himself had been immediately tomahawked and scalped. Why he had been kept alive, he did not know at first, but afterward guessed, from the gesticulations of the savages, that he was to be taken with them to their village, to be tortured for the amusement of the old men and women, the squaws and children.

By day he had been compelled to march rapidly between two Indians, one before him, and one behind, who, by their ceaseless vigilance, rendered escape impossible, and who had goaded him on harshly when his footsteps flagged. Keeping to a narrow trail that passed over mountains whose rocky steeps wore his shoes to shreds, and

lacerated his feet, descending through ravines
and gullies, where he often slipped and fell, his
clothes torn to ribbons by blackberry bushes that
bordered the trail, his waking hours made hideous by the cruelty of his captors, and their
threats with knife and hatchet when he sank to
the earth faint with weariness, and sickened by
despair, there had been many times when he
would have been glad if they had made an end
of him at once.

By night he had lain bound hand and foot
beside the roaring camp-fire while the savages
smoked stolidly when the evening meal was
done, or listened to some interminable story told
by one of their number in their own guttural
tongue, not one word of which was intelligible
to the helpless captive.

More than once, for evening sport, they had
fastened him to a tree and hurled their tomahawks toward him, each of which buried itself
in the tree-trunk less than an inch from his
shrinking form, sometimes even severing a lock
of hair from his head. Again they made as if to
scalp him, and shouted with fiendish laughter
when he flinched involuntarily from the touch
of the cold steel.

With such ferocious pleasantries as these, they

had beguiled themselves, and added to his miseries.

Arrived at the Mohawk River, they took to their canoes, which they had left hidden in a little cove when they had journeyed southward. Crouched in one of these, Mark had recovered in some measure from the terrible fatigue of the trail. On the second evening after embarking upon the Mohawk, they had encamped upon a small island in midstream. He was bound as usual, but after the fire died down, and his captors slept, he had contrived to edge himself stealthily away from the glow cast by the embers, and to roll himself quite into the shadow of a rock. There, unseen, he had rubbed the thongs that bound his hands against a sharp corner of the rock, and little by little had cut them through. This done, he was able to free his ankles, and crawl away to the water's edge.

By this time it was dawn, but the river was still dim under the low-lying mists. He slipped into the water, without a sound, and swam, with what speed he could muster, as straight toward the mainland as he could guess for the obscurity.

Fortunately he was an excellent swimmer, and sapped though his strength was by previous hardships, he gained the opposite shore, and sank upon it, breathless and exhausted, at a point where it was heavily wooded, yet where, by good chance, a little brook emptied itself into the river. Remembering that water leaves no trail, he crept directly into the brook from the river, and sank down upon its stony bed, to recover from his desperate exertions.

There he lay for a short time, but soon the sound of savages cries through the mist made him aware that his escape had been discovered. Then followed an ominous silence, which told him that the search had begun, and he knew that no yard of the river or shore would be overlooked, that the brook would inevitably be found and traversed, and himself almost certainly recaptured. Hoping against hope, he had fled up the waterway as fast as his bleeding feet would permit, and had come to the dairy-house, and to Alison.

"And rare good luck it was for you, my lad," said General Johnson, when Mark had ended, "that my business took me to Captain Butler's this morn, for not all the dairy-houses, and the Alisons in this world could have saved you from Red Fox and his braves, unless myself had been there."

"Indeed, sir, I know that," vowed Mark gratefully.

They were trotting up the driveway at Mount

Johnson now, and Mark saw, with astonishment, how considerable was the place to which he had come. The great house, solidly built of rough gray stone, and trimmed with white, a double row of dormers in its leaden roof, was surrounded by a multitude of offices and outbuildings. A large creek, the Kayaderosseras, rushed in a ravine close by. A cooper's house, a bakehouse, and a grist mill, were clustered together beside this stream with its dam and aqueduct. Beyond these stood a vast barn and stables. On the slope of the high steep hill, Mount Johnson, from which the mansion took its name, was the large Council House, wherein William Johnson was wont to discuss with the Five Nations such matters of import as they brought before him. Tepees were grouped in front of it, and all about the mansion itself, squatting upon the grass, lolling on the doorstep, or lying at full-length in the hall, were hundreds of Indians, making themselves at home in their "white brother's house."

General Johnson threw his reins to a stable-boy, dismounted, and with Mark after him, made his way into the house amid a chorus of grunts and *ughs* from lifted heads—the greeting of his Indian visitors. Among those near the door were Red Fox and his band.

On a sign from Johnson, Red Fox arose gravely from his heels, and striding through the blanketed crowds, followed him up the staircase to the General's office on the second floor.

There, at a table, driving his pen at prodigious speed, sat Captain Peter Wraxall, enthusiastic and devoted friend to William Johnson, and his volunteer secretary, a lean-faced, lean-bodied, be-wigged, and be-powdered gentleman, of a quite surprising trimness, and a look of one who knew his business, and did it. At the entrance of the General, he raised his head, showing a pair of steel blue eyes, overhanging brows, and a countenance which, despite the sharpness of its features, was kindly. He laid down his quill immediately, and arose to the attitude of attention.

"Captain Wraxall," began General Johnson, "I've a lad here, that I'm thinking may be of good service to you. He's been captive to my brother, Red Fox, who has sold him to me for two blankets, a knife, and a roll of calico. Be so good as to write out the order for these, so that Red Fox can get them from the stores."

With greedy eyes the Indian watched the rapid movements of the pen that wrote out for him the coveted order, and without more than a final deep-chested "Ugh," took the paper when it was given him, and vanished from the room.

Johnson spoke again: "The lad's name is Mark Renshaw. He's but a little over fifteen, but he's been trained to the pen and figures. You'll soon discover what more he knows when you get him down to the desk." Then in a low aside, " 'T is plain that he comes of gentle stock, and is not broke to harness. Let him go easy for a few days at least, for he's just escaped out of the hands of the redskins, and he's been hard bestead by them. Best see that he has some proper clothes, too." Then he left Mark to the mercies of Captain Wraxall, and went to his more important affairs.

Holding in his hand the bundle that, by the kindness of Mistress Butler, he had been able to bring with him, Mark waited until Captain Wraxall had hastily finished, and sealed the letter upon which he had been engaged when the General had entered. When it had been placed within the leathern mail-sack which lay upon the table, Captain Wraxall rose, pushed back his chair, and said briskly: "Come with me, now,

Renshaw, and I will show you your sleeping quarters. They are above stairs."

In the spacious attic on the floor above a bed was pointed out to him, and an ancient oak press in which he could stow away his belongings.

"I shall not need you for a full half hour or so," said the Captain, moving toward the stairhead. "Do as you like till then."

Left alone, Mark found himself in a lofty room, lit by dormers, and with one lookout window in the very peak of the Mansard roof. Chimneys of small Holland brick, at both ends of the attic, rose bare through the broad boards of the flooring, and out through the massive timbers that upheld the roof. From the dormers he could see directly across the garden, the ploughed fields, and the Mohawk River with its islands, to the flats and the hills beyond.

He went to the press to put away his possessions. Mistress Butler, knowing him to be bare of every necessity, had put together for him a change of undergarments, and such small articles as he could not decently do without. As to outward clothing, he stood in a pair of Lieutenant Butler's hose and buckled shoes, and was clad in a suit, whole and clean, but assembled from the discarded raiment of three: a threadbare broadcloth coat of Captain Butler's, small-clothes and shirt once worn by Wat, and a vest that had belonged to young Walter. This last would have set far too snugly upon his larger, sturdier frame, had he not been sadly reduced in girth by his late privations.

He had not more than opened the door of the press, when the sound of two voices struck on his ears, the one altogether unfamiliar to him, the other unpleasantly reminiscent. While he stood with bent head, trying to recall where he had heard this second voice, two lads mounted the narrow stairs.

The one in front, John Johnson, bore only enough likeness to the General to mark him as his son. A not unhandsome face, his over-full lips, and prominent eyes, gave hint, even thus early, of those vicious qualities of mind and heart that were to lead him into the dissipations and excesses for which he became noted in adolescence and in manhood.

Directly after him, with the light from the dormer window striking sharply upon his lifted face, came Walter Butler, in the midst of a laughing rejoinder to some sally from his companion.

At the same time that Mark, looking over his shoulder, saw and recognized the owner of the puzzling voice, Walter, in his turn, became aware that his hated enemy of the Black Horse Tavern encounter stood before him.

It has been said of Walter Butler that he never forgot or forgave an injury or slight, however small. Far less, then, would he forgive such indignity as he had suffered at the hands of Mark. One lightning glance furnished him with the pleasing knowledge that disaster had overtaken his antagonist, and that an unlooked-for opportunity to make him smart had presented itself.

For Mark, the disagreeable surprise of seeing Walter was immeasurably intensified by his own changed circumstances. Moreover, purchased as he had been but a few hours since by General Johnson from almost inevitable death, and now bound to his service, as well as by gratitude, he was not free to treat as he should like this other whom he despised, who was evidently under the same roof with himself on the footing of a friend and guest.

For a moment the three stood motionless, John showing by his bearing the astonishment that he felt at finding the attic tenanted by this stranger, and Walter and Mark regarding one another with hostile eyes.

It was John who broke the silence. "Who are you?" he demanded curtly, "and what are you doing here?"

"I am Mark Renshaw, late captive to the Mohawks," was the answer, "and I am here by order of General Johnson."

"Mark Renshaw, captive," echoed Walter, with a sardonic laugh, "and also that same ruffian of whom I told you, John, who fell upon me in open day on Garden Street, when I was in New York of late. Not a fellow to be trusted, I assure you. Best let your father know of it, if you would keep your possessions safe." Having delivered this scurvy shot, he leaned against the chimney, hand on hip, covering Mark with an impudent stare.

Mark turned white with wrath at the outrageousness of this falsehood. Under its influence he forgot all prudence. "You lie," he thundered, "but 't is of a piece with what I know of you already. One expects a coward and a cad to be a liar as well."

"Ho, ho!" jeered Walter, "a blusterer as well

as vagabond, is he not, John? Were he an equal,
I would slap his mouth, for calling me names,
but one does not fight with a fellow who wears
one's cast-off clothes. See you, John, he has on
my ancient vest."

"It is the very same," laughed John, leveling
his gaze superciliously upon the garment, "and
odd enough it sits on him, it having such a look
of you."

"You mistake," asserted Mark, in proud de-
nial, turning his back squarely upon Walter, and
addressing John. "These garments, every one,
were given me by a Mistress Butler, when I came
in rags out of the hands of the savages."

"Good Mistress Butler has the honor to be
my aunt," put in Walter smoothly. "Yon pretty
vest came to you straight."

In an instant Mark had whipped off his coat,
torn off the hateful vest, and flung it into Walter's face. "If it be yours," he cried hotly, "I'll
none of it. And hark you, however I may have
lost in fair apparel since first you saw me, you
have not gained in courtesy, although the beating that I gave you then might well have taught
you to mend your manners."

"I'll teach you yours," retorted Walter between set teeth, disentangling his head from the vest, and with that he sprang upon Mark like a tiger upon its prey.

Reduced in strength though he was by all that he had lately undergone, Mark braced himself against the attack, and stood his ground sturdily.

John Johnson, delighted at the turn that things had taken, for he dearly loved to be spectator at a fight, retreated to the chimney-wall, as a favorable point of vantage for viewing its progress.

If Walter, who had not failed to note Mark's weakened appearance had expected to gain an easy victory over him now, he soon discovered his mistake. Nerved by his anger, Mark fought with all his old-time vigor. It was an iron fist that shot into Walter's face, and brought the blood streaming from his nostrils, they were arms of steel that parried his thrusts, and found him out at every unguarded spot. It was a quick eye and an agile frame that enabled him to gauge and to elude his enemy's clever feints, and swift onsets. The voice of John cheering Walter on, and crying praise at every skilful move of his, was a fresh spur to Mark.

They came to closer quarters, and fell to wrestling for the mastery, and with skill pitted against skill, none could have told for a time who was to be victor, yet bit by bit Mark gained upon his adversary, forcing him toward the stairhead, down the first step, from off the second, and then, by a last vigorous shove sent him hurtling backward down the rest of the stairs, and straight into the arms of a commanding figure that appeared without warning at the stair's foot.

Mark, in shirt-sleeves, with disheveled hair, and burning cheeks, looking down, felt his fury suddenly cooled as by a pail of icy water poured upon his head, for confronting him with stern countenance and blazing eyes was General Johnson.

With stunning force, poor Mark realized the compromising position into which he had been drawn. Snatched but a few hours since from hideous danger, brought as by a miracle to shelter, and to means of honorable livelihood, he had, by what semed a cruel trick of fate, been betrayed by justifiable anger into this hand-to-hand encounter with his rescuer's friend. He stood with sinking heart, yet with what courage he could summon, waiting for the storm to break.

"How now, sir!" thundered General Johnson. "Is it in this fashion that you show grati-

tude and repay kindness? I'd have you know this
lad's my guest. Speak out, and explain your behavior, or, by gad, I'll throw you to the Mohawks to do what they like with you."

Walter Butler's black eyes flashed triumph at
this. Here was keen enough humiliation for his
foe to pay himself for more than one bruise.

John, at the stair-head, whither he had come
to engage with Mark, when he saw that his
friend had been worsted, tarried there with
mouth agape, to see what would be the outcome.

In manly straightforwardness, Mark gave his
reply. " 'T was not meant for discourtesy, nor
ingratitude to you, sir. I owe you too much for
that. It was because of such insult from yonder
lad as no one of self-respect could hear without
resenting it, and with blows. He called me thief
and ruffian, and vagabond, and twitted me with
wearing his cast-off clothes, which, had I known
of it beforehand, should never have touched body
of mine. And this from him, whom I had found,
a few weeks agone, to be a knave and a coward,
was more than flesh and blood could bear. So I
forgot, in heat of anger, what I owed to your
roof. I beg your pardon, sir, yet perhaps, did
you know all that went before, in my place you
might have done the same."

He ended with a note of beseeching in his voice, and General Johnson, looking into the brave, but sorely troubled face turned to his, felt his anger melt. Moreover the truth in Mark's tones, and in his bearing, as he made his excuses, convinced him that the lad had been bitterly tried. A man of acute penetration, and power of reading character, William Johnson was fully aware of Walter Butler's true nature, and he flattered himself that he had not been deceived in his gauging of Mark's.

"It was unmanly of you to twit him with his misfortunes, Walter," he said to that youth, holding him off at arm's length. "The savages had fair traveled the clothes off his back. As for his being thief, and ruffian, and vagabond, that's plain folly. You've only to look in the eye of him to know that he's an honest lad, and a gentleman. Let's have no more of this, my boy."

But Walter persisted in his effrontery. "Could you have seen him in New York street, sir, setting upon me unprovoked," he said, stanching his bleeding nostrils with his delicate lawn handkerchief, "you might not think so well of him."

Mark kindled again at the brazenry of this. General Johnson, seeing, determined to run the accusation to the ground "Why was't you did it, Mark?" he demanded, yet in the tone of one who will see justice done. "One does not set upon another in the public street without reason, good or bad."

"I am neither tale-bearer nor boaster, sir," returned Mark, with lifted head, "but since this fellow persists in his falsehoods, I will tell you why I thrashed him there, and far worse, indeed, than I have now. It was because he was brutally attacking a helpless maid, who had no power to fight him off. I, passing, saw her plight, and gave her what help was needed to free her from him. That he suffered in the doing of it was his fault, and not mine."

"Fie, fie upon you, Walter, to handle a maid roughly," said the General sternly.

"He lies," protested Walter, casting a rancorous look at Mark.

"I pray you, sir, ask the maid herself, if you would know the truth," urged Mark. "She is not far to seek. She is that Alison who called you to my rescue this morning."

Remembering the covert look that Walter had directed toward Alison one evening, when he had thought himself unobserved, remembering Alison's words that very morning when she had urged Mark's release from the savages, General

Johnson was instantly certain of Walter's guilt, yet he thought it the part of wisdom to smooth the matter over, lest worse should come of it.

"Whist, now, you quarrelsome lads," he said suavely, "we'll just let the whole thing drop. Boys'll be boys, and fighting's the very life of them. But in my house you'll have to be keeping the peace. As for the maid, Alison, it's hands off her, Walter, my boy, for I'll look after her as if she were my own lass. You were after trying to snatch a kiss, no doubt, from a wondrous pretty creature, and she boxed your ears, belike, as any modest lass would. Don't say me no, for I know the stripe of you. And Mark, lad, cool your hot blood, and off with you now to Peter Wraxall. He'll set you a task that'll sober you down."

Chapter xv

ALISON sat in her eave room with the monotonous drip, drip, of the rain upon the shingles accompanying the steady movement of her pen. She was writing to Dr. Philip Meadowes, to ask that he would procure for her, from the monies which she was sure that her father had left behind him in his native land, a sum sufficient for her passage home; for though Mistress Butler had offered to pay for her return from her own purse, Alison was not willing to accept this, even as a loan.

There was much to say to Dr. Meadowes in explanation of her present situation, and her letter drew itself out until the rain ceased, and the sun burst through the clouds with a watery gleam. Mistress Butler had told her that Watson, having an errand to Mount Johnson that afternoon, would carry the letter, to be placed in the mail-sack there, and so catch the first post, on its monthly journey south.

She folded and sealed her epistle, and hurried with it toward the barn where, now that the rain was done, she expected to find Watson, saddling his horse for the ride to Mount Johnson.

The path glistened with wet, and she had much ado not to lose her footing on its slippery surface.

Instead of finding Watson in the stable, she saw him at some distance, on his way to the pasture to catch the horse he wanted. She stepped into the barn, therefore, to wait for his return.

Looking idly about her, she noticed that Watson had been spending the hour of rain in sharpening farm implements. A scythe, its handle resting against a bench, turned its keen blade upward, and on the bench lay the whetstone, worn thin by long use.

Alison, observing that the scythe stood none too securely propped, and that its blade was turned out in such a manner that she marveled that she had not stumbled over it when she entered the barn-door, was about to cross to it, and set it at a less dangerous angle, when all at once she heard a low sound that stayed her.

It was the cry of an owl.

Once before, in broad day, she had heard that melancholy call, which belongs peculiarly to nightfall. Could it be that Hooting Owl was near?

Fearing to remain in the barn, yet not daring to leave it, she cast a hasty glance about her for some place of refuge, and concealment. In a dusky corner was a great pile of fodder. She fled to it, and creeping in among the dry stalks as quietly as she could, she drew them close about her. Crouching there, behind the frail shield, she watched the door with anxious eyes.

The call was not repeated, but presently there came that same noiseless darkening of the door-way that she had learned to dread. The Caughnawaga was upon the threshold. The walls of her throat clove together from fright, yet by sheer force of will she controlled the trembling of her body, which, by rustling the dry leaves of the fodder, would inevitably have betrayed her presence.

The barn-door, left open for the sake of light while Watson sharpened his scythe, had let the rain dash in, so that the rough boards of the flooring were drenched. Alison, her eyes fixed upon Hooting Owl in almost unendurable suspense, saw him step upon the wet surface with moccasined feet, slip suddenly, lurch forward, and striving vainly to recover his balance, fall heavily upon the barn floor. Clutching at the air as he fell, his body barely missed the waiting scythe.

Not so his arm. With horror Alison saw the blood spurt from it in a bright fountain where the glittering point entered, and heard the Indian's groan of anguish as he writhed himself free. Never had she been able to endure the sight of suffering in another without hasting to its relief. Moreover, she knew, from what her father had taught her, the terrible danger of that jet-like flow. Ferocious though Hooting Owl might be, intense as was her dread of him, she could not let him remain in his present case without trying to give aid.

Casting to right and left, as a hindrance now, the fodder that had shielded her, she sprang forth.

Well for the Caughnawaga, his life-stream spouting from a punctured artery, that Dr. Blair had instructed his daughter in the use of the tourniquet. She undid her apron as she ran, tore a string from it, and tied in it a hard knot. Lifting the scythe quickly, she set it against the wall where it could do no further harm. She fell on her knees beside Hooting Owl, raised up his injured arm, and propped it with the bench.

Upon the artery, above the gaping wound, she placed the knot, and tied the broad apron string loosely about his arm. She had no stick with which to tighten her tourniquet, but she seized the long slender whetstone, and thrusting it under the muslin string, turned it dexterously.

Tighter and tighter grew the tourniquet, slower and slower flowed the red tide, and presently, under the increasing pressure, was altogether stemmed. Then Alison, her first work done, looked into the face of Hooting Owl, and saw that he had fainted, for he had lost much blood. Lying helpless and unconscious before her, his bronze skin curiously overlaid by an ashen pallor, his breath a sigh, he was, for the time at least, not one to be feared, but simply a human creature, who needed her further aid, for now that his hemorrhage was checked, his wound must be dressed.

She was still on her knees upon the barn floor, cleansing the edges of the gash with her clean muslin apron, when the clatter of hoofs told her that Watson was returning, and shortly after she saw him looking in upon her in astonishment, the halter in his hand, and the gray bulk of Dobbin looming between him and the light.

"Whatever's this, Miss Alison?" he began,

and then stopped, for his eyes growing accustomed to the gloom, showed him who it was, stretched upon the floor, and seeing, he knew why he had come.

"'T is that same Indian, Watson, whom you named as Hooting Owl in Schenectady. He called, as then, and when he would have entered here, slipped on the wet, and fell upon the scythe. 'T is a sad pity it was standing there in dangerous wise to do him such despite." While she told the serving-man this, she was drawing the edges of the wound together as firmly as she could, and binding the arm with her remaining apron-string.

"He is so faint from loss of blood that he must lie quiet for a while," she went on. "Can you not carry him to where he can stay undisturbed until his strength comes again?"

"Ay, miss," he answered promptly, and dropped the halter. Leaving Dobbin to stand patiently at the door, Watson strode to the fodder, and shoved a mass of it into a rude bed. He came back to Hooting Owl and, raising him in his arms, staggered with him to the fodder, and laid him upon it. "He'll do well enough here," he said. "Leave him to me now."

Alison bent over her patient, and untwisted

the tourniquet to see whether or not the fountain would break forth again. Not a drop of blood flowed. Seeing that the tourniquet had completed its work, she removed it from his arm, and was about to go, when all at once she remembered her letter, which the coming of Hooting Owl and his misadventure had driven from her mind. She drew it from her pocket, and held it out to Watson.

"Mistress Butler has said that you will carry this for me to Mount Johnson when you go on this afternoon's errand, James. 'T is for the post that goes to New York, and is on a most important matter. I beg you, take it safely."

Watson saw the shining of a bit of silver that went with the letter, and took both, readily enough. "I'll see it safe there, miss," he said, as he clapped the saddle upon Dobbin's back.

There was a slight stirring in the corner. Hooting Owl moaned. Alison leaned over him to catch his muttered words. "Water," he sighed, "Water."

"Yes, yes," she promised, and swift-footed, she left the barn, and was away to the spring.

No sooner was she gone than Watson hastened to Hooting Owl, and touched him on the shoulder to arouse him fully. It was his wounded member, and Hooting Owl winced with pain. His lids quivered as they opened wide.

Watson's face was close to his; Watson's eyes were fixed upon him with a steel-like intensity. Watson's voice demanded: "The beaver-skins? Where?"

Hooting Owl opened his parched lips, and tried to form clear words in answer, but could not.

"The beaver-skins?" repeated Watson, with merciless insistence. "Where?"

Wearily Hooting Owl made signs.

Watson nodded briefly, to show that he understood, and was back at his horse, and mounting it when Alison returned, carrying a gourd half-filled with sparkling water.

Hooting Owl would have used his feeble strength to seize the gourd and drain it, but as she might have treated an ailing child, Alison put aside his hand, raised his head, and gave him barely as much as would moisten his throat, knowing, as she had been taught, that more, at first, might do harm.

There, upon the fodder, she left him, before long, sunk in an uneasy slumber, filled with dreams that were strung upon a continuing thread of pain.

To Mistress Butler, stitching away at linen wristbands for Lieutenant Wat, she went, to tell of the sad mishap. The good woman shook her head in stern disapproval of the serving-man.

"A careless fellow he is, that Watson. By the scythe so easily might anyone have been killed. And thou, my little one, how clever thou art to know at the instant what must be done! It is his life that Hooting Owl owes to thee. He shall quiet lie until evening. Then together we will go, to see what more he needs, and to take him food."

While the two drew their needles in and out, and Alison told Mistress Butler how her father, partly for her pastime, and partly because she had a gift that way, had taught her much concerning the care of the sick and wounded, James Watson, thinking on the beaver-skins that were to enrich him further, pounded along the road to Mount Johnson. A present of game to General Johnson was fastened to the pommel of his saddle, and Alison's letter reposed securely within the recesses of the saddle-bag.

Arrived at his destination, and having discharged his errand with the game, Watson was mounting the staircase to the General's office to give the letter into Captain Wraxall's charge for the post, when, on the landing, half-way up, he met Walter Butler.

"A letter for the post?" Walter greeted him. "My grandsir's, I suppose. You need go no further, Watson. I'll see that it reaches the mail-sack."

"It's none of your gransir's, Master Butler, but one that I've give my word to put to post myself," and Watson made as if to pass on.

Walter blocked the way. "If not my grandsir's, whose then? Come, Watson, answer."

"Miss Alison's, then, if you must know. Now let me by sir, pray do, for I must get back to my evening's work."

But Walter stood his ground, though he spoke in guarded tones. "You like a good bargain, Watson, do you not?" he insinuated meaningly. "Make a second one with me." His hand went to his pocket, and drew out half a crown. "Give me the letter, and this money is yours. What say you?"

The serving-man shook his head. "No, Master Butler," he replied. "I've give my word."

Walter tossed the half-crown lightly in his hand. "You are a fool, James," declared he.

"The young miss has had hard times enough," muttered James Watson, unwilling still, yet

Walter, watching him closely, saw that under the influence of the money, tossed so alluringly up and down before his eyes, he was beginning to waver.

"Heads you take, tails you leave," murmured the boy, throwing up the coin with an assumption of indifference.

Falling, the half-crown showed the head.

Shrugging his shoulders, as though fate, and not he, had decided, Watson handed over the letter, and took the money.

"Remember, James," was the whispered admonition, "you are to hold a close tongue, and remember, too, that for any other letter writ by this person, I will pay the same price."

Thus it came about that James Watson rode home to find his beaver-skins, with a silver half-crown in his pocket, lying side by side with a silver shilling, and that Master Butler, standing before the fireplace in his bedroom, late that evening, watched a letter consume to white ash upon the embers.

Chapter xvi

ON a fair May morning Alison rode off to spend the day at Mount Johnson. Mark Renshaw had come to fetch her thither upon the General's own horse, Queen Bess.

She was pleasantly a-quiver at the prospect of seeing for the first time, not only the two motherless daughters of William Johnson, but the large mansion as well, with its furnishings and pictures sent direct from London, of which Mistress Butler had told her much.

Even the knowledge that Walter Butler still lingered there, as the welcome guest of John Johnson, could not damp her anticipations. Had not Mistress Butler said that General Johnson kept his young daughters very much retired, in a separate part of the house, with Mistress Stewart, their governess, away from the comings and goings of the Indians, the interpreters, the traders, scouts, and militia-men, who overran the more public rooms? It was altogether unlikely, she told herself, that she would encounter Walter at close quarters.

So, without uneasiness, she trotted smoothly along behind Mark, under the flickering sun and shade, upon the self-same road over which she had jolted uncomfortably in the farm wagon at nightfall not many weeks before.

A bewitchingly lovely picture she made in her frock of cream-colored chintz, its ground sprinkled with bright cherries, its fine lawn tucker drawn demurely down. A light cloak of cherry colored tafettas set off the soft dark curls that fell from under her drooping Leghorn hat, bound under her chin with wide cherry ribbons. Her father had chosen these pretty things for her in London, and had kissed her, and called her "Cherry Ripe" when she had donned them to ask him artlessly if they became her. This morning Mistress Butler had bade her wear them, and Alison had put them on. There was a mist over her eyes as she had tied the ribbons and settled her tucker before the small square mirror, remembering what he had called her.

Mark, waiting for her at the horse's head, had thought, when he saw her come out to him through the gray doorway, that he had never seen any maid half so fair as she. Maria Butler, fastening a trim dust-skirt upon her when she was seated on Queen Bess, had looked on her bright apparel, and declared approvingly, "It is a brave finery, and becomes thee well. Keep close the dust-skirt round thee, that thou mayst come fresh and clean to Mount Johnson, my kleintje."

Alison's thoughts were less upon her attire, however, than upon Mark, and how he did in his new life, and in exchange for what he said of General Johnson's kindness, and Captain Wraxall's strict training of him in the duties of a secretary's clerk, and of what it cost him in self-control to keep a quiet and dignified demeanor when Walter Butler took advantage of favoring circumstances to treat him as an inferior, she told him of Hooting Owl and his wound, and how, when next morning she and Mistress Butler had gone a second time to the barn, thinking to find him still there, he had disappeared, and naught had been seen of him since.

"I trust he came safe home," she said, gravely, "for savage though he be, I would not have him suffer harm."

" 'T was astonishing that a young maid should have known how to check such dangerous bleeding," cried Mark in a burst of admiration. "I would that I knew how to use the device, myself."

"It is easy. I will show you, if you like, when we have opportunity," offered Alison readily.

"How came you by the knowledge?" inquired Mark, half turning in the saddle as they rode.

"My father taught me it, and much else," returned she, with that note of loving pride that always crept into her voice when she spoke of him. "He was a marvelous fine doctor."

"Ah!" sighed Mark, and the reins dropped loose in his hand. "That is what I fain would be, myself, and what, in truth, I might have been had my own father lived. But now there's naught for me but writing and figuring—clerk's business."

Alison was stirred to quick sympathy. "Be that as it may," she said gently, "I'll teach you all I know, and then—there are certain books in my father's chest, concerning medicine and the chirurgeon's art. I treasure them greatly for his sake, but I'll lend them to you one by one to read in if you like."

" 'T is good of you," replied Mark, flushing high with pleasure.

"And be not too discouraged," added Alison wisely. "Who can tell? You may yet have your heart's desire, and come to be a doctor after all."

"So do I hope," declared the lad fervently.

Then Alison was keen to have him tell her of his adventures while in captivity, and so, talking freely and without constraint, as though they had known one another from early child-hood, they came to Mount Johnson. Looking upon the mansion, she recognized it as the place which she had hoped might have been her desti-nation and her kinsman's house when she had passed it a few weeks ago.

It filled her with unbounded amazement to see so great a concourse of Indians gathered about it. Among them she thought she saw at least one face that was not entirely unfamiliar.

"Is not that Red Fox? The one wrapped in a blanket, and sitting under the elm-tree at the foot of the hill?" she whispered cautiously to Mark.

"Yes," he made answer. "Now that General Johnson is once more Indian Commissioner, he has come again to talk over some matters that concern his tribe." He had no time to say more, for they had reached the alighting block, and General Johnson himself was standing there to lift Alison from Queen Bess.

"My girls are fair pining for a little society other than their own," he said, after they had exchanged greetings, and Mark had trotted off to the stables. With that, he tucked her hand under his arm, and brought her to a quiet room in a sunny secluded part of the house, where two girls, somewhat younger than Alison, sat over their needle-work under the instruction of Mistress Stewart. The three rose as the General entered with their guest.

"Here's the lass I promised you," he announced in his full rich voice. "You see she's brought you the fashions from London town. Mistress Stewart, I commend her to your best graces, for so she stands in mine."

Mistress Stewart, a pleasant-faced Englishwoman, with a widow's cap lying sedately atop her cushioned hair, gave her a few words of cordial welcome. Nancy and Mary, in Watteau sacques and quilted silken petticoats, their fair hair flowing, stood back a little timidly, now that they were face to face with this stranger.

"Come, Nance. Come, Mary, You're just all maids together," encouraged their father, pulling them forward, and laying their hands in Alison's. "Get to your chatter, for the day'll be over, and your new friend off and away again before you know it."

He left them then, to their own devices, but it took all Alison's frank sociability and winsome ways at first to break the ice, for the Johnson girls, isolated from others, seeing almost no one but their governess and their father and brother, were as shy as fawns. In due time, however, Alison was teaching Nancy the latest embroidery stitch, at which Mistress Stewart did not disdain to look with undisguised interest. Mary sat beside the cherry silk mantle, where it lay spread out upon the sofa, touching it with delighted fingers, and begging eagerly to be told what they were wearing now in London.

"You may call me Nan," said Nancy, a little later, her reserve quite melted away, "for we are to be great friends, of course. This knitted purse, when it is done," she drew it from her workbasket as she spoke, and spread the needles to display its beauty, "is for Mr. Daniel Claus, a gentleman from the Palatinate, well liked by my father."

"And by yourself as well, Nan, or you would not be so diligent at the task," put in Mary, shaking a roguish head at her; at which Nan pouted and laughed, and owned he was.

"Mr. Claus is a marvelous clever scout," she informed Alison, "and knows the Indian tongues. But not so well as does my father," she added proudly. "'T is said that he could speak,

the Mohawk in two years after he first came to
Warrens Bush from Ireland, and soon thereafter
could talk with every Indian in the Five Nations in his own dialect, as 't is called. There
be few who can do the like."

"The language has a strange sound," opined
Alison. "I heard your father speak it to Red
Fox on the day when he bought Mark Renshaw
out of captivity, and from his lips it fell as it
did from the mouth of the savage."

Happily engaged with these new friends, the
time sped swiftly for Alison, and engrossed in
teaching broidery stitches, and filling greedy ears
with talk of England, she quite forgot the possibility of an encounter with Walter Butler, and
the hope that she had cherished on her way to
Mount Johnson that she might come and go
without being seen by him.

As a matter of fact he had seen her as she
alighted before the door, and had noted the flash
of her cherry-colored mantle as she disappeared
with General Johnson into the mansion. His
keen eye for beauty, wherever he saw it, had
forced from him a reluctant admiration of hers
today.

Now he was apparently loitering about aim-

lessly among the Indians, addressing first one
and then the other with a word or two, where
they smoked with half-dropped lids and stoic
countenances, or sprawled upon their blankets
in the May sunshine. But steadily he drew
nearer to Red Fox under the spreading elm.

Red Fox marked his approach. He knew this
young pale-face, and his ways, and felt no surprise when Walter took a seat upon the grass
beside him, as if to rest awhile, and began to
speak to him in an undertone.

"The chief of the many scalps missed one on
his last warpath," insinuated Walter, with a
side glance at the immobile redskin. "It is not
the way of Red Fox to do so. If he let his captive go unharmed, he must have had good
reason."

Without removing his gaze from the distant
river, Red Fox answered, "When my white
brother, William Johnson, asked of me my captive, I gave him, for Red Fox refuses little to
his friends." Then, with a sardonic smile, he
added, "The price was good that my brother
paid me. Red Fox can spare one scalp, for when
he wishes he can gather ten to take its place."

"Does the great chief know, I wonder, how it

was that William Johnson asked of him his captive?" questioned Walter, watching Red Fox narrowly.

"My brother told me that he needed him to help him in his work for the Indian," returned Red Fox, indifferently.

"But does not the great chief know," persisted his companion, "that it was not so much because he needed him, as because a young girl begged for his life that William Johnson said this?"

Red Fox shrugged his shoulders as though that concerned him not. "My white brother pleased himself in that matter. For Red Fox, the price that was paid him was good."

"Does not Red Fox know," suggested Walter, "that this paleface youth hates the Mohawks for the sufferings that he endured upon the trail, and has sworn vengeance upon them? Is he not where he can do them harm in a hundred ways? He is a liar, and will whisper his lies into the ears of William Johnson, who loves him, and will believe him. Moreover, will not the young white girl, who saved him, help him to take vengeance? She, too, is dear to William Johnson, and for her he will do much. It was for her sake alone that he paid the price that you asked for your captive. Together, these two will bring disaster upon your people. Let Red Fox be wise in time."

A venomous gleam shot from the inky orbs of the savage, and Walter perceived that his words had not been without effect. But it faded, and he answered doggedly, "William Johnson is just to his Indian brothers. He will not listen. Besides, he is my blood brother, and Red Fox has given his word."

Walter drew closer, and his next words were whispered in his companion's ear. "It is true that Red Fox has sworn. But is there nothing that he can do to protect his people from their enemies? Has not the great chief some clan brother, not of the Five Nations—a praying Caughnawaga, perhaps?" he hinted, "one who could do for Red Fox what he cannot do for himself?"

The eyes of the redskin glistened. "Red Fox has such a brother in the clan of the Turtle," he said. "It may be that he will hearken to Red Fox, and carry away this danger that threatens."

"Let not Red Fox wait too long to speak to him," warned the other. "The young girl is here today. This evening, at sunset, he, who was your captive, rides home with her to my grandsir's house. Might you not show them to your brother of the Turtle, that he may surely know them when he is ready to do what you wish?"

"My brother shall see them, and when he is ready, he will not fail to do what Red Fox asks," replied the other.

"It is well that my brother, Red Fox, can reap his vengeance with clean hands," smiled Walter Butler, and rose slowly to his feet. Loitering deliberately as before, he passed to the mansion, there to amuse himself with a book until the return of the hunting party, John Johnson among them, that for his own reasons he had declined to join at their early morning start.

Red Fox sat quiet for a full half-hour, seemingly almost asleep. Then he, too, arose, and walked slowly up the wooded hill, and over its crest, to where a high rock jutted boldly from its farther slope. In the shadow of the rock he stopped, and putting his hands to his lips, uttered a long low call. Once only he gave it, and stood with bent ear waiting.

Soon, from out the silence of the wood, came the mournful cry of the owl at twilight, and directly after a dark shape glided from behind a tree trunk near him, showing him the face of Hooting Owl.

"My brother of the Turtle comes quickly," said Red Fox in welcome, "but not before his brother has need of him."

"Hooting Owl is ready," replied the Caughnawaga. "His clan brother has only to speak, and what he asks is done."

"Let my brother choose his own time," said Red Fox, "but let him remember that danger threatens my people, and let him act as quickly as he can." Then he laid before Hooting Owl the story of Mark's capture, his escape, how he was found again, and sold, and what manner of help it was that the Indian now required of his clan brother.

"Hooting Owl is willing," declared the Caughnawaga, "but he, too, must have his price." He stood impassive, waiting for Red Fox to speak.

"Let my brother name it," said the Mohawk.

"My brother, Red Fox, knows that I have come that I may take back to the Frenchmen news of what their enemies the English are doing. Can Red Fox tell his brother how to find what he seeks?"

"You shall see," returned Red Fox. "Tonight, in the great council room, my white brother, William Johnson, talks with Peter Wraxall and

Daniel Claus. If Hooting Owl will come to me at the elm-tree that he knows of, when the darkness has fallen, I will show him how to go to where he can hear clearly what they say. It may be that he will learn what he wishes to know. Let him stand, also, by the gateway, before the sun hides his face on the other side of the mountain, and he will see the pale-face youth ride by with the maiden behind him. He may know him by his hair, which is like copper when it shines the brightest, and the maid, because her cloak of silk is like the ripe cherries upon the bough."

"Hooting Owl will do as Red Fox bids him," agreed the Caughnawaga. He took from his belt a string of white and purple wampum, and laid it gravely in the hand of his brother of the Turtle. Red Fox dropped the pledge of Hooting Owl about his neck, and they parted without further word.

At the hour when the sun shone level through the trees, turning the earth, and all about it, to gold, Alison and Mark rode forth from the gate on Queen Bess.

Hooting Owl, standing concealed among the shrubbery, looked keenly at the youth from under his narrowed brows, that he might not fail to know him wherever he might find him, but when he saw the maid, the bronze of his cheek grew a shade paler, and he drew far back among the branches, for her face was the one that had looked into his in pity in his hour of suffering, and he knew that it was to her that he owed his life.

Chapter xvii

IN the darkness of a moonless night, Hooting
Owl stood under the deeper darkness of the
spreading elm, waiting for his brother of the
Turtle. He had not long to wait. Out of the
blackness stole Red Fox, and silent as the shades
themselves, the two clan brothers glided away
together from tree to tree, from bush to bush,
until they had almost reached the house. Then
Red Fox paused, and laid a detaining hand upon
the Caughnawaga.

His voice came in a low whisper: "Into the
great chamber William Johnson will come soon
now. The doors and windows will be shut, so
that none can hear him speak except those whom
he wishes. He will draw close to the hearthstone
with Peter Wraxall and Daniel Claus that their
voices may not creep out to ears beyond the
door. But if my brother of the Turtle will climb
up through the chimney that I will point out to
him, he will come out upon the housetop, and
there, at the end that looks toward the setting

sun, he will see the chimney that rises from the hearth where William Johnson will sit. If Hooting Owl will lay his ear to the chimney-top, he can hear all that is spoken in the great chamber below, as clearly as if he sat by the side of the hearth."

"The advice of Red Fox is good," murmured Hooting Owl. "I will follow it."

No further word was spoken. The two resumed their progress, Red Fox leading, till they came to the back of the mansion, and stood before a small window set low in the stone foundation. Its shutter was thrown back.

Red Fox sank upon one knee, and looked cautiously through the opening into a room some twenty by thirty feet, the kitchen of the house. Its massive fireplace still contained the dying embers left after the preparation of the evening meal, but the room was for the time deserted.

Red Fox knew that the chimney that Hooting Owl must mount lay in the cellar beyond, and that in order to arrive at it without being discovered they must be swift.

"Let my brother come quickly," he whispered, rising, and guided him to a door that led directly into the kitchen from the outside of the house. On soundless moccasined feet, the two entered, crossed the stone slabs of the kitchen floor, and passed into the vast cellar, in which stood three yawning chimney entrances, as massive as the one in the kitchen itself. To the farthest of these Red Fox pointed.

Hooting Owl gave a curt nod of understanding, went straight to the chimney, and, without a backward glance at his companion, slipped his naked body through the opening, and began to mount the sooty wall.

Red Fox, his promise kept, departed, unheard and unseen, as he had come, certain that his clan brother would fulfil his part of their bargain as faithfully as he had performed his own.

Up and up the rough inner surface of the chimney, Hooting Owl now climbed, now writhed, and at length stepped out upon the sloping roof. Without pausing to regain his breath, he made his noiseless way to the chimney nearest to the setting sun. Standing at his full height in the darkness that wrapped it round, his ear was just above the level of the chimney-top.

Soon he was able to verify what Red Fox had told him. He heard footsteps enter the room below, heard the doors and windows closed, heard chairs drawn to the hearth, and presently the sound of voices rising. Distinct and clear as though he were in the room below the words came to him.

Across the impassive features of the listening Caughnawaga flitted the ghost of a smile. What reward might he not expect from Onontio, as the Indians called the Canadian Governor, when he returned to Montreal with what he had heard? He stood close to it, listening intently, laying up in that marvelously accurate and tenacious memory of the Indian each ascending word.

Ignorant of the eavesdropper upon his roof, General Johnson was speaking freely of the details of the coming campaign.

"Governor Shirley has pledged Massachusetts for full twelve hundred men with their pay and maintenance, if the other colonies thereabouts contribute their due proportion. The Assembly backs him up. Connecticut votes twelve hundred men. New Hampshire promises five hundred. Rhode Island will send four hundred. New York must furnish eight hundred."

"And yourself to lead them all," commented Daniel Claus suavely, in his correct English, which had, nevertheless, a faint foreign accent, as the sign of his Palatine origin.

"To lead them all," repeated Johnson, a shade of gratified vanity in his voice.

" 'T is no small wonder that Governor Shirley was not eager to snatch at the command himself, being of a stirring habit, a prime mover in the plans against Crown Point from the first," avowed Peter Wraxall.

"Ah, he had his own reasons for looking in this direction," replied William Johnson. "He knew right enough that if a man from any one of their New England colonies headed the expedition 't would rouse the envy of all the rest, and set them at loggerheads among themselves. For success, an outside man was the wise choice. It was easy to see that New York would be flattered to be given the lead, and would back up his project the stronger because of it. Besides that, they must win the Five Nations to stand by them, and no one can influence them so well as I can myself. Of that, Shirley's well aware."

Boastful as this might sound from the speaker, it was a truth as fully admitted throughout every colony from New England to the Carolinas, as it was known to his companions, to the listening Caughnawaga, and also by Canada's Governor, and his Algonquin allies.

"The Iroquois have it in their power to hamper us greatly by standing aloof," said Claus gravely.

"Sure they have," returned Johnson, "but the Council at Alexandria gave me full power to treat with them. Add that to my commission as major-general of the levies of Massachusetts and the other colonies, and you'll see that I've got all the strings in the two hands of me."

"And your first move?" inquired Daniel Claus with keen interest. Hooting Owl leant closer to the chimney opening.

"Will be to call the Five Nations to a great council at Mount Johnson," answered the General. "Messengers will be sent to every tribe without delay, summoning them to assemble here on June 21st. Then I'll find out not only what support they'll give, but I'll sift out the matter of the Caughnawagas, also. The Caughnawagas, as you know, have many kin, who have left their homes in the Mohawk country to cluster round the French priests at Montreal, and these 'praying Caughnawagas,' as they call them, have been let come and go freely among us, and bring their furs down to the traders at Albany."

"True, and many a spy among them has carried news to Montreal, to their Onontio, of what the English do and plan," broke in Peter Wraxall.

"Just that," agreed the General. "They've

been a thorn in the side, and I'm thinking they'll give us trouble now."

The eyes of Hooting Owl narrowed as he listened yet more intently.

General Johnson continued. "With kin among the French forces, our Caughnawagas here will be less than half-hearted in favor of joining us, and no doubt they'll cast their voice against their brothers of the Five Nations throwing themselves actively into the campaign. If they remain neutral, that is all we can hope for, but, by Gad, if they play us false, and join our enemies against us, we'll scotch them like snakes." At this point, Hooting Owl distinctly heard the blow that the General struck the table beside him to emphasize his words.

"Except for the Caughnawagas, General, do you believe that we can certainly count upon the Five Nations?" asked the Palatine.

"To be neutral at least, yes," responded Johnson. "But how many'll go to battle, or fight when they get there, no mortal man can predict, no matter what they promise at the council. Old Hendrick, the Mohawk sachem, will keep his word. He'll bring his warriors, and most of the others, I hope."

"Can we count upon the Senecas?" inquired Wraxall.

"Perhaps so, perhaps not," answered Johnson dubiously. "We shan't know which about any of them till the last minute of time, but it will mean at least six hundred warriors gained, if they join us."

"What is the strength now of the garrison at Crown Point, sir?" asked Daniel Claus.

"Nothing known on that head since the scouting parties of last year reported only a few men, and no life about the fort. But of that, Dan, we'll know more when the scouts come back that I'm sending out tomorrow. I'd like to send yourself with them, but I'll be needing you at the council-fire, and belike you'd not be back in time if you went up the Lake."

"And after the council, sir?" Wraxall queried.

"Getting on the march as soon as we can," was the prompt reply. "A grand rally on the Flats at Albany, and from there straight north. If the New England colonies'll just keep from quarreling among themselves over their commands and their supplies, 't will not be long, and July, and no later, ought to see us heading for Crown Point."

"By way of Wood Creek, sir, I suppose," observed Claus deferentially.

"Perhaps," replied Johnson. "We may find, however, that it's better to go by Lac du St. Sacrament. That'll depend on what we find when we reach the Great Carrying Place. There'll be heavier work than ever now with correspondence, Wraxall. Young Mark'll be a godsend to you there, I'll warrant. Remind me to write Governor Delancey the morn's morning about the supplies from New York, will you? And Claus, if you'll send a runner off to Fort Hunter, to get me Arent Stevens, I'll be obliged to you."

A sound as of a heavy chair pushed back and of moving feet, followed by the creak of an opening door and the slow dying away of footsteps told the spy upon the housetop that the betraying chimney would yield him no further information that night.

He sank down upon the roof and crept softly back to the chimney by which he had ascended. Arrived at the bottom he listened carefully before venturing further. Voices in the kitchen warned him that he could not yet cross it. But his quick eye had showed him before he began his ascent to the roof, where he might secrete himself in such an emergency. Acting as supports to each of the chimneys were arches, five feet high, five feet deep, and four feet wide. These formed capacious vaults used for household stores. Wooden doors closed them.

Hooting Owl opened the door of one, and glided into the darkness of the interior. There, behind a sheltering hogshead, he crouched, until at length, long-continued silence in the kitchen gave promise that he could pass through without discovery.

Pushing open the door of the vault, he saw that darkness reigned in the kitchen also, even the red light of the embers having been quenched under a heavy layer of safe-guarding ashes, before the servants had left the room for the night.

Like a shadow Hooting Owl had come. Like a shadow he departed under cover of the enveloping night, but with him, like a vision, as he journeyed along the trail, went the sweet face of a young girl who had flashed by him beneath the setting sun, the young girl who had come to him earlier, like a spirit sent from Manitou, to save him from impending death.

Chapter xviii

DOWN the dim forest reaches of the Kayaderosseras and Sacandaga trails, thickly
shaded by the rich leafage of late June, along
the broad and dusty road from Fort Hunter and
Canajoharie Castle, from north, from south,
from east, from west, Oneidas, Senecas, Mohawks, Cayugas, and Onandagas, filed gravely
and silently toward Mount Johnson to the
Great Indian Council. Tiederigones, Shanander-
gones, Ogquagas, and Delawares, sent sachems
to join in the deliberations around the council
table. Nine tribes in all answered to the summons of their Commissioner.

Close following them came ragged children
with black elf locks, and a horde of squaws,
their young papooses slung in cradles to their
backs, to squat among the pines and hemlocks
on the hill slope, and watch from a distance the
proceedings of their chieftains and sachems. The
wide flat from house to river, the rising ground,
scattered with tepees and cabins, were alive with

some twelve hundred redskins alone. Added to these were neighboring Dutch farmers, traders, interpreters, scouts, and militia-men from the nine companies of militia of New York under the command of William Johnson.

Near the mansion, under the open sky, a table had been placed, at which sat General Johnson, his secretary—Peter Wraxall, Daniel Claus, Colonel John Butler, Reverend Mr. Ogilvie, who was missionary at Fort Hunter, Arent Stevens the interpreter, and a number of other men prominent in the affairs of the Mohawk Valley.

Rough benches, occupied by the sachems and chiefs of the Iroquois, faced those seated about the table. In wide semicircles beyond these were the young braves and seasoned warriors, ranged strictly in the order of their seniority. Wherever the eye turned, it beheld the blue smoke curling up from the camp-fires of the families who had come with their great men to the council.

All this, and a hundred other details, greeted the eyes of Alison, trotting up to Mount Johnson with Lieutenant Wat Butler on this memorable day. A pressing invitation had been sent to her from the Johnson girls, warmly seconded by their father, to visit them during the council, and view the spectacle from the windows of the mansion. Mistress Butler, content for her own part to remain at home, although she, too, had been urged to come, had put the girl under her husband's care, and called a cheerful farewell to them both from the doorway of the gray house on the hill.

Several weeks had passed since Alison's first visit to Mount Johnson, and in that time the friendship between the three girls had been well cemented; for although General Johnson did not permit his daughters to leave the seclusion of their own home, Alison had been sent for on a number of occasions to bear them company there, coming and going usually under the escort of Mark Renshaw.

To Nan and Mary Johnson her advent had proved a welcome and unexpected linkage with the outside world, from which they had until now been completely sequestered, for William Johnson, mingling freely though he did with his unlettered neighbors as one of themselves, drinking flip and playing cards with the Dutch farmers, smoking and feasting on dog-flesh in the wigwams of the savages, never forgot his own gentle birth nor his kinship to his uncle, the rich Sir Peter Warren, when it came to the society that his motherless daughters kept.

True, their mother, Catherine Weisenburg,

had been a penniless redemptioner, whom he had
first bought to be his housekeeper, and in the end
had married, but his girls were being brought up
with the utmost circumspection under the tute-
lage of excellent Mistress Stewart, as became
their station. It pleased the General mightily,
therefore, to afford them this companionship
with Alison, and she, on her side, found great
enjoyment in the society of Nan and Mary, and
in her chats with Mark as she came and went.

Fortunately for the happiness of this intercourse, Walter Butler had gone home to Fort
Hunter, taking John Johnson with him, a day
or two after Alison's first meeting with the girls,
and this had been an incalculable relief to Mark,
also, who had often been hard put to it to endure in silence, and with self-restraint the in-
nuendoes and underhand meannesses that
Walter dealt out to him, whenever their paths
crossed, and he could do so without danger of
being detected by the General.

Early this morning, however, Alison, looking
from the kitchen window, had seen the two boys
galloping toward Mount Johnson with Colonel
John Butler and his company from Fort Hunter,
and now, as she drew near the mansion, she
secretly hoped that Walter would be too deeply

engrossed by the excitements of the day, and the stir and bustle of important arrivals to give much heed to her own. At present, to her relief, he was nowhere visible.

As she approached the door of the mansion, she saw, for the first time, the sparkling dark-eyed Indian beauty, Mollie Brant. Forming a restless little group around her, keenly interested in all that was forward, were her younger brother, Joseph Brant—a vigorous stripling of thirteen, and Charlotte, Caroline, and William, the half-breed grandchildren of King Hendrick, from Canajoharie Castle. The handsome copper-colored faces, and sharp black eyes of these made a striking contrast to the blond beauty of Nan and Mary Johnson, who gazed out demurely from the drawing-room windows.

These last spied Alison coming, and went at once into a soft flutter of excitement and pleasure, with waving of handkerchiefs, and nods, and smiles, and in a moment more were receiving her affectionately, and vying with one another to give her the best place beside themselves, from whence to look out upon the scene.

"Here, here, by me, Alison," insisted Nan.

"Nay, but she will see better here," urged Mary.

"Best let me stand between," smiled Alison, with an arm about each.

Accustomed as Alison had been from infancy to none but scenes of peace, this concourse of savages and white men that she now gazed upon, brought to her consciousness the grim significance of an assemblage gathered together for purposes of war.

Where on her previous visits to Mount Johnson she had grown familiar with lolling, loafing redskins, wrapped in dirty blankets, she now saw dignified warriors, in ceremonial dress, with grave faces, rigidly erect bodies, and sedate bearing frowning down to respectful silence the faint outbursts of hilarious disorder among the young squaws and children on the outskirts. Under the glare of a summer sun they sat as though graven in stone, listening to William Johnson's first public speech to them as Superintendent of Indian Affairs.

Through the open window, Alison and her companions heard him distinctly.

He spoke in English, so that the white men could understand him, but he used the picturesque phrases and the ceremonial customs of the redmen, and presented a belt of wampum to his allies at the close of each salient point in his speech. He urged them to unite with one another and with him in the common cause. When he had finished, Red Head, the Onondaga sachem, rose and delivered it over again to the Iroquois as it was read to him in a low voice, paragraph by paragraph, in the Indian tongue, by Daniel Claus.

General Johnson then handed a bundle of sticks to the Onondaga, who gave it in turn to a sachem upon the front bench, which drew a wave of loud applause from the assembly, followed by profound silence. When this silence had lasted for some moments, King Hendrick, grand sachem of the Mohawks, arose, and in obedience to a wave of his hand the Council quietly dissolved.

"There—'t is the end for today, and tomorrow is Sunday, so there will be no meeting, Alison, but on Monday the Iroquois will answer. Such long speeches as they make! 'T is as though they never would come to a finish. Father bears with them patiently, for he knows that Indians in council cannot be hurried, and he follows their custom, and makes his speeches as long as their own. But come, now, to the garden. The English daisies are out. Shalt show us that game with the petals. You know the one I mean."

"Nan would try it, thinking of the gentleman from the Palatinate, methinks," teased Mary, enjoying her sister's swift blush. "You know he calls her his little sweetheart."

Alison laughed gaily. " 'T is a foolish game, and means naught," she said, "but one that all maids play wherever daisies blow; and as for being sweethearts, to gentlemen grown, 't is their jesting way to call us that even while we are still babes upon the knee." Thus she covered Nan's confusion.

In the garden closes, behind trimmed hedges of box, the daisies grew in thick pink and white mats of bloom.

"One I love, two I love, three I love, I say," chanted the three in musical undertone, plucking the petals one by one, to drop them with mock solemnity upon the velvet grass, until only the green calyxes were left upon the stems.

"I did name mine for Cousin Guy Johnson," announced Mary gravely, "and see—he loves me."

"How was't with you, Nan?" inquired Alison archly, turning upon Nan.

" 'T was well enough," she said, with an air of satisfaction. "I'll not count another. At least not today. What named you yours, Alison?"

"Indeed I forgot to name it at all, for I was busy thinking on yours," replied Alison.

A laugh ridiculed them from behind the box-hedge. Nan and Mary dropped their daisy heads upon the ground, but Alison held hers stiffly upright.

" 'T is Walter Butler," whispered Nan. "Come, Alison, let's go in, or he will come and tease."

Without a word, and still holding the green stem in her hand, Alison leisurely followed the two in their hasty exit from the garden.

Walter Butler, sauntering away from a spot which promsed no further amusement, came nigh to stumbling over an Indian girl, upon her knees, peering with glittering dark eyes through an opening in the hedge. Plainly she had been watching this daisy game with eager curiosity.

"The white maiden will teach you, too, Bright Waters," he said to her. "It is a spell that all maids practice."

"Bright Waters will learn it then," answered the young Indian briefly, and rising from her knees fluttered away.

But it was not until the day was almost over, that Bright Waters, keeping watch for an opportunity, was able to receive her lesson.

General Johnson, wearied by the business of the council, and seeking refreshment in the evening coolness, had brought Alison out into the garden to show her a rose-bush, lately brought from over the water. Its first buds were just unfolding.

Nan and Mary had begged to join them, but their father had laughingly refused. "No, no, my pretties. I'll have Alison quite to myself for a bit of a while. Away with your pouts. You'll be having her back with yourselves before a half an hour is out." So saying, he had tucked the girl's hand under his arm, and drawn her away, leaving his daughters to amuse themselves as best they could for the time being.

In the garden now, standing before the rose-bush, Alison was crying, "Oh, General Johnson, we had its like in our garden at home. Every morning, while the season lasted, I gathered a bud for father's coat. It was his favorite rose, because it had been mother's favorite first."

"Pluck one for me, Alison," said the General gravely.

With delicately poised head, and graceful fingers, she obeyed him, and he, watching her, seemed to have caught in his keen eyes a little of the trailing river mist that was beginning to drift in across the wide flats to the sheltered nooks of the garden.

He held the lapel of his coat to her, and she drew the rose stem carefully through a loop of the rich gold braid that adorned it, settling the bud daintily to place, and holding back her head to view the effect.

"It becomes your coat," she pronounced, with sweet decision.

William Johnson stretched out a large and shapely hand to the bush, and broke from it the fairest bud that remained. He stripped it of its thorns, and tucked it in among her brown locks. "And this your curls," he said very low, adding abruptly, "There, let's take a turn along the walks, my lass. These roses will bring back too much of England to us, if we linger too long beside the bush."

They had scarcely paced the length of one green alley, before a servant came to bring the General word that Captain Peter Wraxall was obliged to know his wishes in regard to the content of a letter to be sent within the hour to Governor Delancey.

William Johnson's sigh, as he turned about in the direction of the house, had in it a touch of impatience. "I'd not thought our bit of a while would be so short, Alison."

" 'T is too bad," she replied regretfully. "Yet you've shown me the rose, and we have had a few moments' chat, after all. 'T was more honor than I had expected."

About to accompany him, she stopped, seized by a sudden impulse. "Oh, may I not go back alone to the bush, General Johnson, to fetch a bud for Nan's hair, and for Mary's?"

The General cast a searching glance in all directions before answering, but he saw no cause for anxiety, nor for refusing.

"Sure you may," he granted. "It'll please 'em. Don't be long, though."

His firm footfalls died away toward the mansion, and Alison ran back to the rosebush. A bud chosen for Nan, she was about to break a second, for Mary, when she felt a touch, like the brush of a butterfly's wing, on her elbow. Light as it was, it startled her.

Turning quickly, she saw a young Indian girl, clad in a robe of softest deer-skin, embroidered with porcupine quills, dyed in many colors. An embroidered fillet was bound in her ebon hair, and was adorned with a single feather set jauntily aslant above her brow. She held a daisy in her hand, which she stretched out to Alison beseechingly.

"Bright Waters learn too," she said.

Overcome with surprise at this sudden apparition, Alison remained for a moment speechless; but she quickly perceived that this young creature, savage though she was, was nevertheless only a harmless maid like herself.

Unable to resist the pleading look upon the girl's artless face, she proceeded at once to explain the charm.

"Have you named the flower?" she asked, when one point after another had been made clear.

Bright Waters nodded.

"Then say the words after me," commanded her teacher.

Now Alison had opportunity to learn how marvelous is the memory of an Indian. The words that she gave to her pupil for a single time, were immediately repeated correctly by Bright Waters, not once, but several times, and never did she falter, nor make the slightest error, as she drew one daisy after another from her deer-skin pouch to test the charm upon it.

"Bright Waters knows," declared the girl,

when the fourth daisy had shed its rosy petals upon the ground. "She thanks the pale-face maiden, and says farewell."

Before Alison could reply, she had vanished as silently and swiftly as she had come.

With sudden realization that Nan and Mary might be wondering at her long absence, Alison hurried from the garden with her rose-buds.

The Indian girl, climbing the slope to her father's tepee, stooped to gather a handful of the common white daisies of the American fields.

"Bright Waters can make magic with these," she murmured with a contented smile. "She does not need the flowers of the pale-faces."

The young girl had believed that her lesson in the garden was known only to herself and Alison. Nevertheless, two others had observed her there: Walter Butler, and Red Fox.

"Do you not see that it is as I told you?" whispered young Butler to the bent ear of the savage. "The young white girl works magic, but the magic of this paleface, that will bring good luck to her, will bring misfortune to the redman. She is teaching her magic to Bright Waters. Let Red Fox beware."

The eyes of the chieftain were as the flint when the spark flies from it under the stroke of the hatchet. "Bright Waters is the promised bride of Chief Red Fox," he muttered hoarsely, "but let her not work upon him the bad magic of the paleface, lest she should feel his tomahawk."

"Then let Red Fox see to it that the young pale-face maiden is carried away soon, if he would not have Bright Waters learn more and more of this dangerous magic," urged Walter.

Chief Red Fox drew proudly away from the hand that Walter had laid upon him, and prepared to leave him.

"Let not my white brother fear for Red Fox," he said haughtily. "Bright Waters will obey him when he speaks."

He strode rapidly away, and overtook Bright Waters with her flowers in her hand.

"What is it that Bright Waters learns of the young pale-face?" he demanded, without other greeting. His tones were harsh.

The maid looked up at him, and saw the thunder-cloud on his brow. Mischief seized her. She shrugged her shoulders, and choosing a daisy, began to strip it of its petals, whispering meanwhile, in a tone too low for him to hear, the words that Alison had taught her.

Red Fox blazed to fierce anger. "Let not

Bright Waters trifle when she is asked a question. Let her speak so that Red Fox can hear."

Bright Waters saw that she must give answer, and some time, of course, when he was not angry, she might tell him the secret that the blossom held, and, also, that she had named the flower for him; but not now. Nor would she stay with him to quarrel. She slipped past him as he would have caught and held her, and called back to him mockingly over her shoulder as she fled, "Squaw's magic, Red Fox! Squaw's magic!"

Chapter xix

IT was the last day of the Great Council. Alison had listened from the windows of Mount Johnson to strange words, and had looked out upon deeds that were stranger still. Many times in the man who was at the head and front of that council, she could not recognize her friend. Except that his skin was white, and his native tongue the same as her own, she would have taken him for a savage of savages.

She had heard him say, before all the Five Nations: "My kettle is on the fire, my canoe is ready to put in the water, my gun is loaded, my sword is by my side, and my axe is sharpened. I desire and expect you will now take up the hatchet, and join us, your brethren, against all our enemies." This did not surprise her. She realized that it was necessary to win the Iroquois to an active upholding of the campaign. She had heard William Johnson say more than once to his white friends that the one hope of defeating the French in their attempts at conquest, the one hope of maintaining the integrity of the colonies, and keeping them free from French rule, lay in securing the unswerving adherence of the Five Nations to the English cause, and in keeping them as a dreaded bulwark thrown across the boundary that separated the territories of the rival powers. That living bulwark once broken, or once turned, to let in the tide of French invasion, would, he declared, be an irreparable disaster, and he, as a patriot, would spare no pains to bind the Five Nations solidly to their present allegiance.

She was aware, from all that she had heard, that it was because he spoke their tongue, followed their customs in his dealings with them, mingled with them as one of themselves, received them as their brother and generous benefactor, judged them justly, that they loved and venerated him, and were loyal to him as a whole. He it was, indeed, and he alone, who was able to hold them to the British as permanent allies.

But when she saw him throw down the war-belt, and saw him, streaked with paint, begin the hideous Indian war-dance, crouching and leaping, yelling the blood-curdling war-cry, brandishing hatchet and tomahawk around the great war-kettle, by the blaze of the fire at night, a veritable savage, reveling with savages, she covered her eyes in haste, and turned away shuddering from the gruesome spectacle. It was as though she could not bear it, and it took all his fatherly kindness to her, all his courteous consideration, his dignity, and tenderness, in the very few moments in which she saw him each day, to win her away from the memory of those other moments in which she had seen him in the fearsome dance.

After many days, many speeches, many belts of wampum given and received as pledges, and as enduring records of words spoken, the Nations, now Six in number, gave their promise, on June 28th, to follow the General whenever he should call them to battle. Red Head, great sachem of the Onondagas, who had been nominated spokesman of the Nations during the council, had departed; Nockie, great sachem of the Ojibwas, had said farewell; Hendrick, head of the Mohawks, was gone; and as it was with them, so it was with the rest. Alison and her young friends had seen them, one by one, winding away over trails and open road, carrying with them guns, new and old, powder and ball, corn, strouds, blankets, and presents. And with their departure, the heavy burden upon William

Johnson of feeding and feasting nigh upon two thousand hungry redskins of boundless appetite was lifted.

Only the matter of the Caughnawagas remained. This obstinate tribe had prolonged the council for fourteen days, trying secretly to persuade the others to come out in favor of the French. On the other hand, efforts had been made to win over the Caughnawagas, or at least to obtain their promise to keep out of the battle; but the delegates who had been sent to them for the purpose, came back having gained nothing.

The time came when the patience of General Johnson was exhausted, and he was compelled to say: "The Caughnawagas are at present looked upon as friends, and treated by the English as our brethren: they come now freely and unmolested to Albany, and the soldiers have orders to treat them civilly, and as friends. We have no desire to spill a drop of their blood. But if they will be obstinate, and act as enemies against us, you cannot blame us if we treat them as their headstrong rashness will deserve."

Meanwhile Hooting Owl came and went, learning much from Red Fox, and sending it on by many channels to his Onontio, at Montreal. But in giving aid to his brother of the Turtle,

Red Fox did not fail to remind him of his promise to rid the Mohawk Valley of Alison, and of Mark, and to urge him to keep that promise soon.

"The pale-face maiden has taught squaw's magic to Bright Waters," he complained, his eyes smoldering with hate, "and it will bring misfortune to my lodge."

"Let my brother wait a little longer," advised Hooting Owl. "I will surely carry the maiden away captive, but it is not wise to do so now. When William Johnson has taken the war-trail northward, and she is defenceless, then Hooting Owl will do as he has promised, and she shall see the Mohawk country no more."

So Red Fox, writhing though he was under the enforced delay, and angered and made uneasy by the mischievous behavior of Bright Waters, was obliged to allow Hooting Owl to do as he thought best.

With the closing of the council, Alison had returned to the Butler roof. Walter, hot with indignation because he was not to be allowed to go upon the campaign, although he urged that Joseph Brant, who was no older than himself, was to be permitted to go, had accompanied his father to Fort Hunter, there to remain. General

Johnson, engaged day and night in gathering men and stores, journeyed back and forth between Mount Johnson and Albany, chafing under the delays of the New England colonies, who were bickering among themselves, as had been foreseen, over their allotments of fighting men, and the supplying of army stores.

Mark Renshaw was tied to Captain Peter Wraxall's elbow, whose pen seemed never to flag, nor to permit that of his assistant to rest. Yet Mark throve on the busy life, and the excitement in the air, and one day in July, sent on an errand to old Captain Butler, he found time to make known to Alison the proud news that he was to go north with the fighting men.

"You see," he told her, in a ringing voice, "Captain Wraxall cannot be spared from the field. He must be there to write, and send dispatches, and he has urged that I be allowed to go and help him as I do at Mount Johnson. At first the General would not hear to it. He declared I was too young for the duty. But when he looked me up and down, one morning lately, he saw fit to change his mind, for he said I was more sound and well set up than many of the young men who are encamped upon the Flats at Albany."

"Oh, Mark!" cried Alison, in great concern, "you are brave, I know, and strong, too, yet you are but a lad, after all. Perhaps—perhaps—if you go away, you may never come back."

"As to that, no one can say, indeed," returned Mark soberly, "but this I know: if I should die, it will be for my country. To help and defend that, I am willing to give my life."

"But if you should be carried captive—" she demurred, her eyes shadowing to a deeper gray.

"I shall escape," affirmed Mark boldly. "And if I cannot, then I must bear what others have borne. You would not have me be a coward, Alison."

"No, no," she exclaimed in haste. "Surely not. Indeed, that you could not be. 'T was but a moment that I feared. I am proud to have you go. When must it be?"

"Captain Wraxall has said that I must be ready to go at any time. It may be in a week; it may be sooner."

"Then I must give you something to take with you. One can never tell—it may save your own life, or that of some other. Wait here, Mark." Leaving him standing on the graveled path, the reins over his arm, she ran into the house.

"What is it, my Alison?" called Mistress Butler from her loom, hearing her flying feet upon the stair.

"Something for Mark," she answered, and hurried on, to fall upon her knees beside her father's chest. She took out a small physician's case, leather bound. It was equipped with stores for emergencies, whether of wounds or sickness.

Alison held it to her breast for an instant, her head bent. "It is for Mark, dear father," she whispered, a tremor in her voice. "He goes to battle. I know you would have me give it."

Back with Mark, she pressed it into his hand. " 'T is father's little case," she said. "There are in it many things that may serve you well. Take it with you when you go."

"Nay, you should not part with it, Alison," objected he. "Since it was your father's, it is uncommon dear to you."

"Ah, but you must take it," insisted she, and closed his reluctant fingers over it. "It will comfort me to know that you have it. Besides, the books that I have lent you, and that you have studied with such prodigious diligence, will have taught you how to use many of the things that it contains."

Mark let her have her way. "I shall feel myself almost a doctor, having so fine a case to carry with me," he smiled, placing it in his saddle-bag with care. "But this is not good-bye, Alison. I shall see you and Mistress Butler more than once, I doubt not, before I go."

"Still, if it should be that this is good-bye, and who can say that it may not be?" replied Alison with sober face. "God bless you, Mark, and grant that you come safe back again."

"God grant it," returned he, grown very grave, "God grant it, Alison, and keep you in safety, too."

He vaulted into the saddle quickly, and was gone.

He had not thought that it would be farewell, certainly, and yet it was.

Two days later he was riding toward Albany, with Captain Wraxall, to be ready to go northward from thence, the moment that the order to march was given.

Red Fox, encamped with the warriors of his tribe, on the broad Flats above the little Dutch city, saw him coming while he was still far distant, and remembering the promise of Hooting Owl, never doubted that the bullet or the tomahawk of a Caughnawaga would surely find him before the campaign was done.

Chapter xx

"YOU will give it to Watson with your own hand, Alison, will you not?" begged Nan.

"That I will," promised Alison, taking the little parcel that her friend confided to her.

"It provokes me that it was not complete before Mr. Claus went away," complained Nan, with disappointed face. "I had wanted much to see how it looked when 't was made fast to his great gold watch. But all the tiny beaded patterns did take me such a weary while. 'T is rarely pretty, now that it is done. I hope it pleases him."

"It cannot help but please," was the encouraging response. "Never have I seen any fob so handsome. You have outdone yourself, Nan."

"The parcel should have a red riband about it to set it off rightly," said Nan regretfully. "But I had not so much as a scrap, nor had Mary, nor yet Mistress Stewart; so this narrow strip of scarlet list must serve, since it is the proper color."

" 'T is pretty," commended Alison, touching the scarlet knot lightly.

"You'll bid Watson take great care of it, and deliver it without fail," Nan besought her anxiously. "I want that Mr. Claus should wear it, like a gage, you know, Alison, such as ladies gave their knights in olden time."

Alison laughed blithely, but kissed her, too. "Never fear, Nan, it shall reach him safely, if words of mine can avail," she assured her.

August was nearing its end. News had come back that General Johnson was still at the Great Carrying Place, waiting for stores, bateaux, and re-enforcements to come up with him. James Watson had been recruited as a wagoner, and was to leave next morning with a party of others, conveying provisions for the forces, and he it was who must see that the gewgaw upon which Nan had spent so much time and pains reached Daniel Claus.

In confiding her parcel to Alison, Nan had exacted a promise from her that none but James should know of it, and she sent a bright shilling piece with it, to pay him for his trouble, and ensure his carrying out of her commission.

When Alison returned to Mistress Butler, therefore, under the care of Pieter Brouck, she gave her the niddy noddy reel that she had been sent to procure of their neighbors at Mount Johnson, but made no mention of the beaded watch guard tucked away in the depths of the velvet pouch that swung at her side.

She was still awaiting an opportunity to give it to James privately, when Mistress Butler came to her with a basket. "See, kleintje," she said, "I must have tart apples for my apple-cakes. Wilt thou not fetch me some from the orchard?"

Welcoming the prospect of being out among the long, cool orchard rows on this sultry day, Alison took the basket, and went directly to the tree that Mistress Maria most favored.

A breeze from the south stirred the silver green leaves overhead, and swung the great yellow apples to and fro on stems seemingly too slender to bear them. From this tree, and now from that, breaking in upon the continuous rustling of the leaves, came the rush of a falling apple through the foliage, and its heavy thud as it struck the earth.

A hugh sphere tumbled to Alison's feet. She stooped to pick it up, but just as her fingers were about to close upon it, she felt herself suddenly seized from behind, in a grip that stopped her breath. The arms that prisoned her, and dragged her upright, were dark and sinewy. Relentless hands closed her mouth, lest she should scream for help, and while she struggled vainly to free herself, to turn and see who pinioned her, a bandage fell over her eyes, was tightly drawn, and knotted at the back of her head.

Terrified, unable to make the slightest attempt either to escape, or to cry out, she felt herself half dragged, half carried along, whither she could not guess. That she was in the power of Indians, she was certain, but whether they were Mohawks, perhaps Red Fox and his band, or roving Caughnawagas, or Algonquins, enemies to the British, she had no means of knowing. Half fainting, a sick trembling in all her limbs, she was hurried constantly forward.

Her feet began to catch in roots, her hair was jerked by briars, she felt the whip-like blows of slender branches upon her cheeks and neck, and heard crisp sounds as of pushed-back leaves. By this she knew that she had left the orchard, and was being borne along a forest trail.

Half dead with fright, she went on thus, for what seemed to her to be many hours, and until, from the creeping chill in the air, and by the dampness arising from the moldering leaves, she felt that night must be drawing on. In all this time, not a syllable had been spoken by her captors. In silence she had been seized; in profound silence she was compelled to go onward.

It was not until even fear had been driven into the background by benumbing fatigue, that she was brought to an abrupt halt. So unexpected was this that her knees gave way under her, and she would have fallen, but for the hands that still securely held her. By them she was lowered to what, from its velvet softness, seemed to be a bank covered with moss.

Snapping of sticks, and then sounds of twigs rubbed briskly together, made her surmise that a fire was about to be made, and presently sharp crackling and streaming warmth convinced her that she had guessed rightly.

Comforting though it was to her shivering body, the overwrought child recalled stories of torture that Walter Butler had taken delight in telling in her presence, and she recoiled from the horrid possibilities of this fire in the forest. In veritable agony of spirit, she prayed for courage, for strength, for deliverance.

She felt a hand laid upon her hair. She shrank from it shuddering, lest it should be the dreadful forerunner of the scalping knife. Then, as she had feared, came the cold touch of steel, and with a leap of the heart, she gave herself up for lost. But the stroke of the knife was to sever the thick folds that had blinded her. These fell away, and in the ruddy light of the fire, that served to make the night shades of the forest blacker by contrast, there were revealed to her two Indians. The one was unknown to her, but in the other she recognized Hooting Owl.

Hooting Owl, stooping, fettered her ankles with stout thongs of deerskin, but to her surprise, neither of the Indians made any move to do her harm. They allowed her to remain undisturbed upon the bank where they had placed her when their rapid march had come to an end.

Upon a piece of bark torn from a near-by birch, they poured a little heap of parched corn, and placed it beside her; in a folded leaf they gave her water from the brook, and when she had eaten and drunk what she could, they made for her a bed of pine boughs. When this was done, they laid her upon it, bound hand and foot, leaving her no possibility of escape. Silent still, these two sat by the fire smoking, their pipes filled with strong tobacco, and though Alison's lips were now unsealed, she did not dare to ask whither they were taking her, nor what was to be her ultimate fate. She only lay tense, and watchful, fearing to sleep.

The deep quiet of the forest, pressing heavily upon her ears, was broken occasionally by the padding footfalls of some prowling wild beast, or call of night bird, and once Alison heard the cry of the great horned owl. It was as the voice of her captor. Looking through half-closed lids at him, where he sat smoking interminably beside the fire, Alison thought of how he had once lain helpless, and at death's door, and would have passed through it but for her. How was it that he could be so ungrateful, had so soon forgotten his debt?

The time came when, in spite of herself, she dropped into uneasy slumber, and when she awoke the fire was no more than dying embers, and the sun was up. Hooting Owl still sat motionless, his pipe between his lips, but his companion had departed with the early dawn.

Alison, stiff with the night chill, and the hampering thongs, stirred miserably upon her couch of boughs.

Hooting Owl laid down his pipe gravely, rose, and coming to kneel beside her severed her bonds with the knife from his belt.

"Let not the White Rose of the Mohawk be afraid," he addressed her. "No harm shall come to her. Did she not save the life of Hooting Owl when he lay wounded? Could the redman forget his deliverer, or repay her ill? Do not think so. It is to save the White Rose from her enemies that he has brought her here, and will take her on to a place of safety."

Astonished at his words, yet reassured by the gentleness of his tone, Alison looked at him inquiringly.

"The White Rose has two enemies who never rest," went on Hooting Owl, "the young pale-face, Walter Butler, and the Mohawk chief, Red Fox. The White Rose may not know this."

Alison answered him without hesitation. "I know that Walter Butler is my enemy. I have never harmed him, but he has injured me, and because a brave lad punished him for it, he hates us both. But Red Fox has no cause to bear me ill-will."

"He would not say so," returned Hooting Owl. "Because the White Rose pleaded with William Johnson, he lost his captive. He believes, for so Walter Butler has told him, that she works against his people; and besides—has not Bright Waters, who is to be the wife of

Red Fox, learned squaw's magic from the White Rose? This, he believes, for so Walter Butler has told him, will bring misfortune to his lodge."

"Squaw's magic?" echoed Alison, puzzled. "What can that mean?"

"Bright Waters has learned to take a flower, and to scatter its leaves upon the ground, saying strange words beneath her breath, that Red Fox cannot hear, and while she says them she will not look at him. When he asks her what they are, and what they mean, she laughs at him, and says: 'Squaw's magic, Red Fox. Squaw's magic.'"

In spite of her perilous situation, Alison was moved to smile at the superstition of the savage, and the teasing spirit of Bright Waters. "I have taught Bright Waters no magic," she said. "It is but a game that children and young maids play."

"Red Fox believes what Bright Waters tells him," replied Hooting Owl, "and so he hates the White Rose. Yet, because of his promise to William Johnson, he dares not harm her, but he has made me, his clan brother, promise to take her away forever from the Mohawk."

"Forever!" exclaimed Alison, and her voice rang hollow.

"Yes," declared the Caughnawaga. "The White Rose goes with me to Montreal. There I will give her to the good Sisters, who will receive her, and make her one of themselves. In their care the hate of Walter Butler and of Red Fox cannot reach her. In this way Hooting Owl can keep his word to his clan brother, and can repay the White Rose for saving his life."

Alison heard him, appalled. Once given over to the French nuns at Montreal, what hope had she, an English girl, of ever seeing her friends again? Those friends passed in a slow-moving procession through her thoughts: Mistress Butler—always kind, and wondering now what had become of her; General Johnson—it would be long, with him away upon the campaign, before he learned that she was gone from the Mohawk; Nan, and Mary—she knew that they would be grieved; and Mark—Mark, her first friend and defender in a strange land. England, and its people, her own dear old friends there, had seemed too far off, now that the war was on, to be reached by her for many a day to come; but these others had quickly become so dear. In spite of Walter Butler's enmity, how happily she could have stayed among them until the time came when she could be got home to Kent.

Now, to gratify the malice of a wicked and vengeful boy, and the hatred of a superstitious and resentful savage, she was to be exiled not only from her own country, but from the friends that she had won in this new land. The knowledge of it overwhelmed her.

But what was this that Hooting Owl was saying to her?

"Let not the White Rose grieve," his voice went on. "Is she not more fortunate than the pale-face youth, her friend? It is true that she will see the Mohawk country no more, but a Caughnawaga bullet will surely find the youth before another moon is gone."

"Before another moon is gone."

The words stabbed her. She saw Mark in fancy, as he had stood that last day, when, without knowing that it was so, he had said farewell. She saw the sunlight striking a glory from his ruddy hair, saw his strong young figure, erect and alert for action, heard his voice vibrate when he had declared, "This I know: if I should die, it will be for my country."

He was to die, Hooting Owl had just told her, his fine young life snuffed out, yet not for his country, but merely to gratify the hatred that his very virtues had aroused in one who was evil.

She could not bear it. She pressed her hands hard upon her eyes, as though by so doing she could shut out the cruel thought from her mind.

Hooting Owl touched her arm. "The White Rose must eat. Before the sun looks through the second bough upon yonder oak, we must be upon the trail."

Eat she could not. Food would have choked her. She shook her head, and turned away.

The Caughnawaga did not urge her. He satisfied his own hunger with parched corn and water, as on the night before, and then arose.

"We are far from the Mohawk," he told the girl, who still sat with drooped shoulders, her eyes close-covered. "The White Rose cannot find her way. She must go where Hooting Owl leads her, if she would not be lost in the forest, and die of hunger, or be torn to pieces by wild beasts. Let her rise now, and come."

Alison knew that it was as he said. In a stricken silence, she rose and followed him.

Chapter xxi

A WEEK passed, and still Alison journeyed with Hooting Owl upon the narrow trail. Avoiding, thus far, both the Kayaderosseras and Sacandaga trails, familiar to white men as well as Indians, and often used by them, Hooting Owl had chosen this obscure one, known only to the Indians themselves, that he might run no risk of meeting Dutch or English settlers, who might capture him, and rescue the girl. And they had gone solitary, and with almost no words spoken, the savage always a foot or two in advance, his sensitive ear keyed to the faintest variation in the girl's footfall or in her slightest movement. It was as though she were surrounded by a cordon of watchers, instead of being preceded by this single, sinuously gliding form, that never faltered, nor erred in its progress.

Sometimes, when her lagging feet, or her panting breath upon some long-continued, sharp ascent proclaimed her utter weariness, Hooting Owl went slower or stopped for a little while to give her rest, but aside from that, their march was broken only for sleep at night, or by pauses for food and drink by day. Parched corn and water, varied by such fish as Hooting Owl took from streams beside which they had their evening camp, was all that was offered to satisfy hunger. Each night Alison lay bound upon her bed of boughs, while the Caughnawaga, seemingly forever sleepless, watched beside the blazing fire.

Knowing full well that the perils of escape were greater than those that now beset her, the girl made no attempt to flee. But whether she rested or went on, in rain and mist, under darkened skies, or through dappled sunshine and freshening breeze, along the borders of sharply dropping precipices that made her head swim dizzily, or over mountain-tops, and down leafy slopes that quickened her pace whether she would or no, she sent up many an ardent prayer for deliverance. From whence it might come in this wilderness of unbroken virgin forest she knew not, but she tried to hope and believe that it would.

Early on the morning of the eighth day, rounding a sharp bend in the trail that ran here along the side of a deep ravine, there burst suddenly upon her unprepared vision, a noble expanse of silver-blue water. As far as eye could reach, and beyond it, the lake stretched away, its surface hemmed in by lofty mountains, whose undulations, and slopes, covered with primeval forests, lay purple, and blue, and moss green, and rose, under the soft mists that trailed their skirts along them beneath the mounting sun. Countless charming rocky islands, green with pine and birch, and hemlock, dotted the mirroring surface of the crystal flood.

Hooting Owl stood still, and pointed to it proudly, with outstretched arm. "An-di-a-ta-roc-te!" he proclaimed sonorously. "The Lake-That-Shuts-Itself-In. The Black Robes at Montreal call it Lac du St. Sacrement. It is over its waters that Hooting Owl must take the White Rose to safety."

To safety! With an almost unendurable pain Alison thought what that safety would mean for her. Such a little while ago, standing with General Johnson in his garden one evening, she had confided to him her bitter disappointment at having had no reply to several letters which she had sent to Dr. Philip Meadowes, telling him of what had befallen her father and herself, and begging him to procure and send to her the money necessary to provide for her return to Kent. The General had consoled her, had taken Dr. Meadowes' address, and had assured her that he would himself write a letter to him sending it in such a manner, and under such conveyance as to make sure that it would reach him, as evidently her own, by some mischance, had not.

"And, anyway, dear lass," he had said, "when there's good opportunity to get you home, under some safe wing, what's a bit of gold between you and me. Sure, I'll pay it from my own pocket in a minute, and welcome to you."

But she had protested that she must not put him to expense; that there were monies in England belonging to her father that would serve her needs.

Of what avail now would be the letter that he had promised to send? And as to dear Mistress Butler, how consumed with anxiety must she be at her sudden disappearance, never to be explained. Poor Nan's parcel could not reach now the one for whom it had been so affectionately prepared.

Hooting Owl aroused her from her distressing thoughts. "Let the White Rose tarry no longer to look upon the lake. She will see it again many times, for she will journey upon it for many days."

Within the hour they were close to its shore, and the Caughnawaga, pushing his way through bushes along an overgrown trail, brought her out to a sheltered cove, thickly scattered with water weeds, and heavily overhung by sweeping birches.

Arrived here, he sought and found a birch-bark canoe that he had cunningly concealed from view some weeks before.

Alison, looking upon the frail bark that was to convey them both over the broad bosom of the lake, with all its possible perils, would have quailed before the impending voyage, however happy might have been the fate awaiting her at her journey's end. As it was, a crushing weight of despair bore her down.

Instictively her right hand went to her pocket to the one thing, except the clothes she wore, that had in it any link with the life and the friends that she was leaving. It was Nan's little parcel, bound with the strip of scarlet list. Many a time she had almost lost the pocket that contained it, by reason of the roughness of the way.

She took out the tiny parcel, and turned it over in her fingers. It was long since she had wept. Her first intense grief for her father had passed into a deep and quiet sense of loss and tender cherishing of his memory and teaching, and of whatever had been his. Except for this love and memory, so vital to her, she had nothing with her that had ever belonged to Matthew Blair, but having these she had all. Largely for his sake, but in part because it was intrinsically her nature to do so, she had borne herself with a cheerful courage during her sojourn in the Mohawk, trying to be his "laddie-lass," and to trust in God's protection and watchful providence. She did not weep now, but she looked down upon the parcel in her hand with dim eyes, passing a trembling forefinger back and forth across the list that bound it.

Hooting Owl, on his knees by the waterside, turning over the canoe to drain it from the water, did not observe her. Neither of them, for the moment, was aware of anything but that which separately concerned them.

Suddenly they were aroused by blood-curdling whoops at their very ears. Hooting Owl, before he could leap to his feet, was set upon and seized by a pair of redskins who began at once to bind him with green withes, so that he was unable to stir hand or foot. Alison, confronted by a third, was made instant prisoner.

Paralysed with terror, plunged from one misfortune into another yet more appalling, the poor child saw the hideously grinning face of the savage close to her own, and his stone tomahawk brandished above her head. Believing that her end was come at last, she dropped her lids involuntarily, that she might not see the weapon in its swift descent. To her swooning sense came the sound of furious crashing through the underbrush, cracking of branches, snapping of twigs —other savages, so she believed, come to join in the work of diabolic cruelty.

Great beads of moisture sprang cold upon her forehead; her heart pounded as if to burst her body. Her fingers tightening convulsively upon the parcel that she still unconsciously held, she waited for the blow that was to bring death. Waited through what seemed an eternity, yet in reality the tomahawk had not had time to fall when a voice rang shrill from the thicket. "Hold, Anawasit, hold! It is the friend of General Johnson whom you are about to kill!"

The words penetrated but obscurely to Alison's comprehension in her fainting state, yet the voice was strangely familiar. Anawasit heard clearly. At the all-powerful name of William Johnson, the arm that pinioned her relaxed, by a fraction, its steel-like grip.

Lifting her lids feebly, Alison perceived that the tomahawk remained poised.

"Do not strike!" shouted the voice again, insistent, and imperative, and Alison knew it for that of Mark Renshaw. Mark's self it was, who cleared at one bound, now, the entanglements of the underbrush, and rushed to where his friend quivered in an agony of suspense.

"If you destroy this maid," he cried, laying a bold hand upon the redman's arm, "William Johnson will surely destroy you."

"The white youth jests," laughed Anawasit, incredulously. "Is not this girl with Hooting Owl, the Caughnawaga spy? Is she not on her way with him to bring news of us to our enemies?"

"No, no," protested Mark, "you are mistaken," and snatching up Alison's right hand, he lifted it before the gaze of the savage. "Behold the sign!" he exclaimed, "the scarlet list! Has not General Johnson ordered us to respect it wherever it is seen? Has he not told us that whoever bears it is a friend? Hooting Owl has carried her away captive from the Mohawk, or she would not be here. Loose her, and when you have brought her to General Johnson, you will learn that he prizes her as if she were his daughter."

But as Anawasit, unwilling to lose his victim, still demurred, authority arrived in the person of Daniel Claus. He had left the camp that morning, taking Mark with him, to go a little way with the party of Indian scouts who had surprised Hooting Owl and Alison. Coming somewhat more slowly in the rear of the party, because of observations that he was making of the slopes and of the shore, he had heard Mark's shout, and the sound of his rush forward, and these had brought him in haste to the scene. Hooting Owl was known to him of old, and Alison he recognized instantly.

"Release the maid, at once, Anawasit," he commanded, and Anawasit was forced to give obedience, grudging though it was.

Then, while Alison, trembling with joy at her unlooked-for deliverance, tried to answer with some coherence Mark's rapid questions, and give him a fragmentary account of her abduction, and how it had come about that she had, unconsciously to herself, possessed the sign that

William Johnson had ordained should guarantee safety to his friends, Daniel Claus strode to where Hooting Owl stood submissive, and bound, before the remaining Indians.

"Bring the Caughnawaga to General Johnson, and see that he does not escape by the way," he said curtly. It was his hope that under the astute questioning that Hooting Owl would undergo from the General, that some information might be gained in relation to the movements of the French.

The party set out for camp, Daniel Claus in the lead, with Alison and Mark close at his heels, and Hooting Owl, with a watchful Indian in front of him, and one behind, bringing up the rear.

Reminded presently of her charge, of which, in the rush of painful circumstance, she had had no opportunity to think, Alison stretched out Nan's parcel to Daniel Claus, saying, "Oh, Mr. Claus, this parcel is for you, a gift from Nan Johnson. It was she who bound the list about it, because she lacked a riband of the color that she desired."

"It was well for you, Alison, that she lacked it, and chose the list instead," said Daniel Claus, accepting the parcel with a gratified smile. "A good Providence guided her fingers to this little strip. Nothing else could have done you such good service. But for it, and Mark's quick eye and action, Anawasit would surely have killed you with his tomahawk before I could have reached you to prevent it."

He undid the parcel, and took out the watch guard. Folded about it was a tiny note, in Nan's carefully exact, yet childish hand. He read it with a softening of the eye, and then tucked it away in an inner pocket of his coat. The beaded fob he hung to his watch with solicitous care.

It pleased Alison to see how it was received, and she was resolved that Nan should hear of it, no less than of the service that the fastening had rendered to herself.

For perhaps a quarter of an hour they traveled thus, and came out then upon a wider trail that crossed theirs obliquely, and passed into a forest of pitch pine. Under a light spatter of rain they followed this until they reached a recently cleared space, thickly sprinkled with stumps of new-felled trees.

Here Alison saw spread out, with a marsh densely overgrown with alders and swamp maples at the right, and a low hill rising at the left, the blue sweep of Lac du St. Sacrement at their rear, the tents of General Johnson, and his army of less than three thousand men.

In spite of some two hundred wagons that came jolting into the clearing over a rough road, the regiments of soldiers and bands of Indians that filed in, the heavy artillery, bateaux, flat-boats, and stores that lay heaped upon the shore of the lake, she realized that an air almost of leisure pervaded the camp.

By way of the lake, which Johnson had lately renamed Lake George, in honor of his sovereign, it was the General's intention to start for Ti-conderoga and Crown Point, but it was plain that neither the men at arms, nor their commander, felt any need of immediate haste.

Daniel Claus led the way directly to a large tent. Its flap was fastened back. Before a table, spread with diagrams and maps, sat General Johnson, in company with General Lyman and Captain Peter Wraxall.

The scout entered the tent, with Alison and Mark directly behind him.

At the slight sound of their entry, General Johnson raised his head. Had a thunderbolt fallen from a clear sky at his feet, William Johnson could not have been more astounded than he was at the sight of Alison in this place, and in such case.

He pushed back his diagrams, and sprang to his feet.

"Child!" he cried, throwing out his hands in dismay. "What brings you here?"

At this, the reaction from her long strain, and recent shock, came for Alison. Essaying to speak, she could not, but tottered, and would have pitched forward, had not the General caught her in his arms.

"Water, Mark, quick," he ordered brusquely, "and then fetch me Lieutenant Wat Butler."

He put Alison into a chair, stroking her head in fatherly fashion. "Poor little lass," he said, "you're fair worn out. Take your time. Take your time."

Chapter xxii

IN the tent that, by General Johnson's orders, had been erected for her beside Lieutenant Butler's, Alison sat that evening, looking out upon the lake.

The General had heard the story of her misfortunes when she had regained her composure. In telling it she had made plain to him Hooting Owl's reasons for saving her life, but she could not tell him, for she knew nothing of it, the price that Red Fox had paid for her abduction.

William Johnson's eyes had flashed dangerously when he learned that the Mohawk had played him false, but when Walter Butler's part in the transaction was revealed to him, he, being thoroughly familiar with the suspicious and superstitious nature of redmen, could understand the treachery of Red Fox, in thinking of the way in which Walter had played upon his weaknesses. As for the boy, he knew that he was resentful, he had seen occasional evidences in him of actual cruelty, but whether he had done this thing in hot blood, or with cold and remorseful malice, the General found it impossible to believe that he could have fully realized, in this instance, the sinister lengths to which Red Fox would go under the influence of what had been told him. He found it the more impossible, knowing that Walter was well aware of his own peculiar affection for Alison. The old, long-standing, intimate friendship between the Johnson and the Butler families would in itself forbid that any one of them should do an evil turn to the other. A boy's irritation, a few ill-considered impulsive remarks made to the savage, would be sufficient to account for all that had afterward occurred, without Walter being deeply to blame. At least he would believe it to be so, until he had proof to the contrary.

Alison had been told in the morning that she would be sent, under escort of soldiery, to the newly begun Fort Lyman, at the Great Carrying Place, to go from thence down to Albany, with wives of soldiers, all to be sent out of camp forthwith. Arrived at Albany, she was to be got back to Mistress Butler in care of a trusty messenger.

The child's heart was filled with gratitude to God for her great deliverance. She remembered her dream, many months ago, in which her father had taken her in his arms beside the troubled waters, and had encouraged her to step into the frail bark on their margin. He had said, "Go forward, my dear, my brave laddie-lass. The Lord is with you. There will be safe crossing." How true his words had been! How often out of extreme peril she had come into a path of safety.

As she sat musing thus, an Indian runner bounded into the clearing, and disappeared into the General's tent. Instantly there was a stir in the camp, and men began to gather in knots, talking in low and excited tones, keeping curious eyes meanwhile upon the tent door.

In a little while Mark came out, and crossed toward Alison, but his progress was hampered by soldiers and wagoners, who insisted upon knowing the cause of the Indian's haste. When at last he reached her, she saw that he was greatly disturbed.

"Silver Heels, the runner, has come in," he told her, "and, Alison, I fear you cannot go in the morning, after all. He has brought word that a body of armed Frenchmen are traveling from South Bay toward Fort Lyman. Poor Colonel Blanchard! He has but a scanty force there to defend it. Volunteers have been called for, to carry him warning."

Alison's cheek blanched. "He will be in sore peril," she said.

"Ay," returned Mark. "I would I were older, that I might volunteer, and be allowed to go."

"He who goes takes his life in his hand, I doubt not," whispered Alison.

"Ay," said Mark briefly, "that I know."

He had no more than spoken when a man, with set face, and the bearing of one ready for desperate hazard, strode into the General's tent, and almost immediately out again. He snatched at a horse, cast saddle and bridle upon it, vaulted to its back, and was off at a dash in the gathering dusk.

His hoof-beats pounding upon the road came to their ears.

Mark spoke again. " 'T is Adams, the wagoner. A rare brave man, all say."

As they sat talking in low tense voices of what the fate of the little garrison at Fort Lyman might be, Wat Butler came to reassure Alison.

"The danger is not for us here, but for Colonel Blanchard, cut off, with but five hundred men."

Nevertheless, as she observed the grave faces of the soldiers, watched the careful posting of the sentries, and listened for long hours afterward, as she lay awake upon her narrow cot, to the pacing of the guard before her tent, Alison could not but wonder what the morrow might hold in store.

Waking from the light slumber that came to her near dawn, she crept to her tent door, and raised the flap. The sun was rising in pale glory from behind the far-off mountains, dissolving the mists that overhung the lake and drifted slowly past the green slopes and shoulders of the nearer hills.

Before his tent, General Johnson stood in earnest converse with his officers and King Hendrick, the wise old Mohawk sachem. Of what they said, she could, of course, hear nothing, but she saw old Hendrick, who was very fat, stoop down heavily, and pick up a single stick, and break it. Again he bent, and putting several together showed that joined they could not be broken. Afterward she learned that it had been a council of war, and that General Johnson had favored sending out a thousand men in two detachments, five hundred to march toward Fort Lyman to cut off the French on their way thither, and five hundred toward South Bay, to catch them on their retreat. Hendrick had opposed him, and proved his point by means of the sticks. Johnson had been quick to take the hint, and agreed to have the thousand go to Fort Lyman in a body. Hendrick had shaken his head, declaring that if they were to be killed, they were too many; if they were to fight, they were too few. Yet, in spite of his opinion, he was determined to join them, although he was too old and fat to go on foot.

From her place, Alison saw the intrepid chieftain climb upon a gun carriage, and heard the stirring tones of his voice as he addressed the Iroquois. Presently she saw him clamber down, and mount a horse, brought for him by the General's orders, and as soon as his warriors could make themselves ready, he rode off at the head of his column of two hundred greased, painted, and befeathered Mohawks.

These had not long departed when she saw a regiment, Colonel Ephraim Williams in command, march out of camp, followed shortly by a second, led by Lieutenant Colonel Whiting.

Alison looked after them, her spirits weighed down by anxious forebodings, and wondering in what manner they would return.

Mark, coming to inquire for General Johnson how she had passed the night, found her sitting with drooped lids, buried in thought. Believing that he knew the cause, he sought to cheer her. "Be not too greatly troubled, Alison. 'T will be contrived to get you to the Mohawk in some way, and out of this dangerous business."

"It's not that, Mark," replied Alison, shaking her head. " 'T is that I am here, a lass, and thus naught but a care to the General in the midst of these grave matters, when I would fain be a lad today, and take my share of what's forward."

Mark looked at her where she sat, the sweetest maid his eyes had ever looked upon, and his voice rang warm. "I would not have you a lad, Alison, for all the lad's work that you could do."

Before Alison could reply, there came from the distance the rattle of musketry.

"They're met," exclaimed Mark, swinging on his heel toward the sound.

"Hark!" breathed Alison, a hand on his sleeve. "Does it not come nearer?"

They listened. Clearer, louder, more ominous, was borne to them upon the morning air, the noise of the firing.

" 'T is a retreat!" cried Mark, in consternation. "Mayhap it means there'll be fighting here, and we not ready!" And then, "Come, Alison, to the General's tent. He'll say what's to be done with you."

"With *me!*" echoed Alison, with a brave lift of the head. "Think not of me, Mark. I'll bear what part I can in this. Haply I can at least hand balls and powder to the men. Meanwhile I'll stay here, out of way."

She had but said it, when Wat Butler hurried in to bid her keep herself close.

Mark rushed away to duty, and soon she saw him flying hither and thither, helping the soldiers in their work of preparing a hasty defence, for until now there had been none, and even the trees and bushes at a few yards in front of the camp, which would afford excellent shelter for approaching enemies, had been left standing.

In a moment the camp had become the scene of frantic activity. Axes rang vigorously, hewing down trees for a barricade, hacking away tangled thickets, slashing down the high growth of fern and bracken. Bateaux, wagons, trunks of trees, piled end to end in a single row, rose rapidly as a rude breastwork before the camp, from the southern slope of the hill on the left to the marshes at the right. Cannon were planted, three to command the road that descended from the pine forest, one upon the very crest of the hill. This work went on in hot haste, for none knew how short the time might be before the enemy would be upon them.

Alison caught fleeting glimpses, now of Lieutenant Butler, now of Daniel Claus, now of Mark, among the surging mass of men. Head and shoulders above the majority of the toilers moved the commanding figure of General Johnson, exhorting, cheering, encouraging, directing them. She recognized another, whom she had first seen in the General's tent, General Lyman, and she thought that there could not be a braver face, nor more fearless bearing than his.

A curiously unsoldierly and motley array it was, that bent every nerve and muscle to erect as speedily as possible this frail barricade. Farmers and farmers' sons they were, most of them, fresh from the fields, the majority without uniforms, clad in homespun, without bayonets, depending upon hatchets instead, carrying the guns and powder-horns that they had snatched from their own chimney-pieces, when they left their New England farmsteads. These worked side by side with the militia, who were equipped with proper uniforms, and accoutrements.

While all strained, and toiled, and sweated

in the heat of desperate endeavor, the sounds of conflict drew ever nearer. Within an hour and a half from the time the relief party had left camp, they began to pour in again, defeated. Fugitives, redmen and white, stricken with terror, hurled themselves in, careless of all but their own safety. After them, more slowly, came others, a pitiful company, bearing such wounded as they had been able to rescue from the deadly ambuscade that had been set for them three miles away, by Dieskau and his Canadian and Indian allies. Colonel Ephraim Williams had been killed in that "bloody morning rout," shot through the brain while he tried to rally his men, and lead them to rising ground. King Hendrick was slain, bayoneted by a renegade Iroquois as he fell from the horse that had been shot under him.

Now, led in masterly retreat by Lieutenant Colonel Whiting, the main detachment came marching in compact ranks down the road, and so into camp.

It was not these that concerned Alison, nor the five hundred sent to guard the flanks of the camp, nor those, who lying behind logs and inverted bateaux, or upright behind the wagons, prepared to meet the oncoming foe. It was to the wounded that her heart went out, in a wave of comprehending pity. Surely here was work for her to do.

She did not hesitate. Snatching the sheets from her bed, she made them into a bundle. From her breakfast tray she caught up a knife. Straight through to the suffering men she went, slipping past the soldiery, who, in that hour of stress, hardly knew that she had passed. But in her going she encountered Mark. She gave him a swift word.

"My father's case—fetch it," she begged.

Mark vanished, and returning with the case presently, found her bending over a poor fellow, binding his gaping wound with strips cut from a sheet that she had brought.

"Stay and help me, if they will let you," she entreated.

"I have got leave to do so from Captain Wraxall," answered Mark.

"Tear me strips like this, then," and she handed him the sheet, already partly used.

Coming upon the girl at her self-elected task, Surgeon Williams, brother to the Colonel lately slain, noted with amazement the deftness and skill with which she was turning a bandage about a wounded limb.

"Who taught you that?" was his abrupt question, as he leaned over a fainting lad to stanch the stream that poured from where a bayonet had pierced deep.

"My father, sir—Dr. Matthew Blair," spoke Alison, without staying her swift fingers.

"Go on, my girl. You're here by God's mercy."

So Alison had found her place, and through the long hours of that dreadful day, she labored without ceasing, unconscious of self, careless of fatigue, and beside her, giving whole-hearted and increasingly efficient aid, stood Mark.

When their work began, the white-coated ranks of the French, their countless bayonets glittering like icicles in the sun, together with hordes of painted Indians, were bearing down upon the little force of sixteen or seventeen hundred rustics, few of whom had ever seen battle till that hour. It went on in the midst of onslaught after onslaught from Indians, who rushed with frightful war-whoops from the woods to leap upon the barricade, where some who guarded it, untried and panic-stricken, would have fled before them, had not the officers, swords in hands, kept them to their posts under threat of instant death if they should attempt retreat.

Cruel echoes of the fray came to the devoted workers among the wounded. After every raking round of grape from the artillery upon Dieskau, deploying before the camp, and answering with firing of musketry from his compact platoons, injured men were brought to the ministrations of the surgeon and his aids. Early in the day General Johnson was wounded, and was carried groaning to his tent to be dressed there.

Alison turned white at the news. She could not trust herself to speak.

" 'T is but a flesh wound in the thigh, they say," whispered Mark, consoling her. "He must lie quiet, though, and General Lyman has taken his place in command."

At first their labors were conducted in the open, with bullets whistling past their ears, or spattering like hail around them, and more than once a shell exploded almost at their feet. Later, for the safeguarding of the wounded, they withdrew, with Surgeon Williams and Dr. Pyncheon, to shelter behind a log-house. There, out of the furious firing, they went on with their work of mercy.

It had seemed as though Mark, his ruddy hair

" 'T is but a flesh wound in the thigh,"
whispered Mark, consoling her.

shining in the sun, had been for a time at least, the peculiar target of one especial Indian among the enemy's forces. Had Alison seen this persistent marksman, she would have thought him strangely like the one who had been with Hooting Owl on the day that she had been abducted from the orchard. But his unavailing fire was cut short at last by a Massachusetts rifleman, and the Indian had made one leap in the air, had given one piercing cry, and fallen dead immediately.

After such a burst of shot as seemed a veritable rain of fire, word came to Alison that a dying wagoner prayed for speech with her. She went with the surgeon's aide, and lying on the ground, close against the log-house wall, his face haggard and drawn with agony, she found James Watson.

The restless seeking in his eyes was appeased when he saw her, and putting forth a shaking hand to clutch her dress, he pulled her down to him. "Miss Alison," he whispered feebly, "I can't go without telling you. Young Walter's got your father's money and papers. I seen 'em plain one morning—in the barn—where he was handling of 'em. Don't rest, miss, till you've forced your rights out of him."

Bewildered at this unexpected revelation, in such a place, her mind and heart distracted from all that concerned herself by the suffering and tumult everywhere around her, Alison seemed to the dying man almost as though she doubted him.

"Oh, miss," he gasped, "it's truth I'm telling you. He's got 'em sure."

Alison wiped the heavy damp from his brow with a compassionate hand. "I do believe you, Watson," she said softly. "Ay, and I thank you from my heart."

"You forgive me, miss, for not telling of it sooner?"

"Yes, yes, indeed," she granted quickly. "But rest you, Watson, rest you. You must not spend your strength so."

In spite of her remonstrance, it was as though he would have told her more, but deadly weakness overcame him, and he was forced to sink back, with closed eyes.

Alison was compelled to leave him thus, and go back to her post. Once there, so constant was the pressure of her ministry to the men brought in a steady stream from where they had fallen before shot and bayonet, that the importance to her of what James Watson had told her was driven far into the background of her consciousness.

Four hours long General Lyman directed the battle, marvelously preserved in the midst of so hot a fire that the smoke rolled in pillars around him. Thunder of cannon, rattle of musketry, continued without respite. The unceasing rapid flashing of the powder blinded like lightning.

Suddenly a tremendous shout rent the air.

Alison and Mark exchanged swift glances. Was it triumph for their own side, or defeat? And if defeat? Ah, they dared not think of what would follow.

But the shouts were those of Lyman's men as they sprang out over the rows of logs to victory, chasing their enemies with hatchets and butts of guns, while Frenchmen, Canadians, Indians, scattered like deer before them in wildest confusion.

General Dieskau, wounded and bleeding, propped helplessly against a tree, was run through a second time, and by a renegade Frenchman, before, on his own demand, he was carried to General Johnson's tent. There, by

William Johnson's orders, the wounds of the vanquished commander were dressed before he would allow his own to receive attention.

But of all these matters, and of the final rout of Canadians and Indians as they rested by the brink of a pool in the forest, by a scouting party of backwoodsmen from Fort Lyman, neither youth nor maid caught more than such a babel of joyful tumult, and such flying rumors, as gave them to know that the victory was to their own side.

Thus the Battle of Lake George was fought and won.

In this day, of the most frightful conflict, the English losses in killed, wounded, and missing were two hundred and sixty-two, most of them being lost in the ambush of the early morning. The French had suffered a loss of two hundred and sixty-eight men, with nearly all their officers, and almost half their troops killed or wounded, for these had borne the brunt of the fighting. General Dieskau bore testimony to the bravery of his foes, saying later that, "In the morning they fought like good boys, at noon like men, and in the afternoon like devils."

Far into the night the little band, toiling for the relief of the wounded, and the comfort of

the dying, stayed at their posts. More than once
Alison had been urged, and even commanded,
by Surgeon Williams, and entreated by Mark,
to leave the piteous scene, and go to the rest that
her wan face betrayed her need of, but it was as
though she could not go while anything remained that her hands could find to do.

She had cause to be glad that she had stayed,
for at last, poor Wat Butler, lifted in arms mar-
tial, yet tender, was brought from among the
fallen to get what help, if any, there might be
for his grievous wound. At first, it seemed as
though there could be none, and Alison, kneeling
beside him, giving him drink when his parched
throat clove together, wiping away the thick-
gathering damp from his icy brow, listening to
his broken, whispered messages to the wife he
so dearly loved, was grateful that she could do
for him some small service, at least, for all the
kindness that he and good Mistress Butler had
shown to her in her extremity. Yet, after many
hours, the almost unbelievable came to pass:
under the skill of Surgeon Williams, and her
own gentle ministrations, Lieutenant Wat
slowly rallied from the terrible collapse that
had presaged imminent death. Watching the tide
of life ebb back in him again, Alison sent up

fervent prayers of thanksgiving to God that her dear Mistress Butler was not to be bereft of her heart's treasure.

Watson died, his own misdeeds against Alison still hidden in his breast, although naught but utter weakness had prevented his full confession. It had been his honest intent to tell her all.

In the confusion of the battle, while the men behind the barricade fought in reckless disregard of all but the enemy before them, Hooting Owl had contrived his escape. Making his stealthy way through the forest, he came upon the scene of the ambuscade that Dieskau had set for the early morning scout. He passed with indifference the men who lay dead upon the rising ground, and in the hollows, but when he came to where Hendrick had fallen, he paused, for close to the aged sachem lay a form that he knew well. It was his brother of the Turtle, rigid in death, his distorted countenance made more ferocious and forbidding by the war-paint that covered it.

The Caughnawaga looked upon him with stoic calm. "Hooting Owl has done his best to save the White Rose of the Mohawk from her enemies," he muttered. "One of them has gone his way to the happy hunting grounds. But she has another, the young pale-face, who still lives. Hooting Owl can do nothing to protect her from him. The Manitou of the White Rose must guard her."

With this he took the trail to where his canoe still lay by the waterside, and embarking in it, he paddled rapidly northward through the night mist that veiled the tranquil bosom of the lake.

Chapter xxiii

MISTRESS BUTLER, at her spinning-wheel, was getting ready the yarn for the winter's weaving. Back and forth, back and forth she trod, with an even graceful movement, drawing the wool, and winding it on the broach of the rapidly turning spindle.

When the broach could hold no more, she reached for her hand-reel, that she might wind the yarn off into skeins. It was with a sharp pang that she took up the niddy-noddy, remembering how Alison had fetched it for her from Mount Johnson, on that August day, and soon after had gone at her request to gather apples in the orchard, and had not returned. That she had been carried away by roving Indians, there was scant room to doubt, but whether she had been murdered by them, or was still living, although in captivity, was shrouded in uncertainty. Even if she were yet alive, Mistress Butler felt that there was little hope of seeing her again. She mourned her almost as though she were her own child, and she could not rest until every means of recovering her had been exhausted. When Wat came home from the campaign he must do what he could, and through every possible channel, to learn what had become of her, for all her own inquiries had come to naught.

Yet, in the fortunes of war, he might be away for some months, and in the meantime, what might not Alison be suffering.

Sighing heavily, Mistress Butler wound off her knots and skeins to the curious waving motion of the niddy-noddy, wishing with all her heart that the war was done, and her Wat home again. The frosts of September had touched maples and birches, oaks and hickories, to red and gold and russet. In a few weeks more there would be snow, and the difficulties of inquiry and search would be increased a hundredfold.

A faint stirring in the room, behind her, meant to Mistress Butler that Calista, her work at the cheese press finished, was coming to mend the fire in preparation for the mid-day meal.

Without turning her head, she said to her, "Thou wilt set me the bake-kettle the coals over, Calista, to be made hot for my biscuits, and put the skillet close over for the pork and apples to be fried."

It was not Calista that gave answer. A voice

that she loved, and had feared that she might hear no more, called to her tremulously, "Mistress Butler," and breaking, called again, "Dear Mistress Butler."

The skein of wool dropped in a heap, in hopeless tangle, from Maria Butler's fingers as she whirled to the sound, and holding wide her arms, cried aloud, "My kleintje! 'T is my kleintje come home!"

Alison ran to her, and was gathered to her breast. In a rush of feeling too deep for speech, they stood thus for a little, close clasped.

Then Maria Butler, with a shaking hand, stroked the dark curls back from Alison's face, and looked inquiringly into the gray eyes, that held in them a strange something, a sort of pitying tenderness, but what was its cause she was unable to fathom. Yet whatever it was, the child would soon make it clear to her.

"Sit thee down, my little one," she said, her hand fastened upon Alison's as though she feared to let it go, feared lest her dear maid should vanish like a wraith. "Here, on the settle, thou wilt tell me from beginning to end everything."

There, where on her first coming to the gray house on the hill, so many months ago, she had sunk down terror-stricken and weary, Alison now seated herself, and with her fingers still locked in Mistress Butler's, narrated all that had befallen her. Of Wat Butler she spake as yet no word. Although she knew it was herself who must break the news of his disaster to the loving woman by her side, who had, as yet, no thought nor feeling but sincere rejoicing at her own return, it was as though she could not utter the first word that would unseal the fountain of distress and anxiety but rather that she must hover, waiting, until such question as Maria herself should ask, would make possible some gentle approach to the ill tidings.

It was not long in coming.

"And sawst thou aught, perhaps, of my dear Wat?" queried Mistress Butler eagerly, when Alison's tale concerning herself was done, and the good woman had expressed her mind as to the punishment that should be meted out to young Walter for his misdeeds.

"Yes," answered Alison, with eyes down-dropped. "I saw him often while I was at the lake."

"And he was well and sound?" urged Maria. "Tell me of him, little one—all that thou canst. Thou knowest how it is—that I hunger to hear."

"In the beginning," said Alison softly, "he was as when you saw him last, well, and sound. But after the battle——"

"Yes," breathed Mistress Butler anxiously, bending closer. "Quick, quick, my Alison! After the battle, what?"

Spurred on by Maria's words and whitening face, Alison made haste. "There had been hard fighting, dear Mistress Butler, and he had been at the very front of it. And so—nay, do not be so sorely alarmed—'t is true indeed that a Frenchman's bullet gave him a well-nigh mortal wound, and that he recovers but slowly, yet Surgeon Williams promises that he will surely be altogether himself again before many months have gone."

Her first terrible fear lifted, Mistress Butler sank back limply upon the settle, the tears of relief raining down her cheeks. Her Wat had suffered, must still, perhaps, have much of pain to bear, but at least he had not been taken from this world, he would come home to her.

So, with Alison's loving arms about her, she listened intently to every detail of his painful illness, asking many questions, receiving her husband's tender messages, and making plans for his comfort at his home-coming, when he should be able to be moved so far, and over such rough and dangerous roads.

Captain Butler, unbending somewhat from the attitude of haughty sufferance which he had maintained toward Alison ever since William Johnson had claimed her for his friend, demanded from the girl the story of his favorite son's experiences, nor did he disdain to learn from her at first hand the happenings of the Battle of Lake George.

Alison, forgiving the hard old man much in his time of distress, patiently repeated over and over to his insistent ears all that she had seen, and all that had come to her through other eye-witnesses of the events of that fearful and bloody day. She told him, also of the death of Watson, but she made no mention of what he had revealed to her concerning the long-lost packet, for Captain Butler had given her no reason to believe that he would mete out justice to her, and she was unwilling, at this juncture, to lay a feather's weight upon Maria's heavy burden.

There came a day, however, when Mistress Butler, sitting over her wool-carding, laid down the last fleecy roll, put aside her cards, and sitting idle, with folded hands, a rare thing for

her, said, "And thou, my poor kleintje, I had
thought thou couldst have been got to thine own
home before this. Hadst but thy father's packet,
now, thou couldst be from these Butlers and
their unkindness free. Thou hadst best let me
give thee the money that thou needst, though I
should miss thee sorely, little one, so much I
love thee, if thou shouldst go."

Then Alison told her all the truth as she had
learned it from Watson as he lay dying.

Maria Butler spoke hotly: "And Walter has
kept it from thee! Has done thee this wrong
also! Out upon him, for a wicked lad! But we
shall have it from him, my Alison, on the word
of Maria Wemple."

" 'T will be a hard matter," replied the maid
sadly. "Watson is gone, and even if there were
any to prove true what he told me, who is there
who can force Walter to give me back my own?"

"His father and his grandsir will do nothing,"
granted Maria Butler, "for they have black
hearts, like his own; but there is General Johnson. He will know how to get it from him. A wise
man he is. 'T is well for thee, my kleintje, that
thou hast for thy friend the wisest, most powerful one in the Mohawk."

So the matter rested during some weeks, for

the colonial forces still lay in camp, with **General Lyman** impatiently urging immediate departure for Crown Point; and the wounded Johnson, tediously confined to his tent, and unwilling to yield command to another, pleading the necessity of holding and fortifying his present position, and the lack of sufficient stores to enable him to proceed. Meanwhile the French came down and strongly garrisoned Crown Point, and the yet nearer Ticonderoga, greatly increasing thereby the task of the British when they should be ready to proceed against them. Nevertheless, for the time at least, the invader had been repulsed, and to General Johnson, in his tent, came the praises of his sovereign, and a baronet's commission.

Tidings of these honors reached the gray house on the hill, and Alison made haste to rejoice with Nan and Mary over their father's good fortune.

Though there might be dissensions in camp, and let her heart at home ache as it would with longing for her Wat, Maria Butler, true housewife of her day, neglected none of the season's duties. Rolliches and head-cheeses were duly made, and carefully seasoned and stored upon cellar shelves that Wat, when he returned, might partake. The vats and bins and hogsheads were filled, the jars and crocks of preserves and pickles were prepared for winter use. From garret to cellar floor, every corner was cleansed and thoroughly overhauled. Her busy hands and watchful eyes were constantly employed, for she knew that only in that way could she keep herself from an unendurable dwelling upon her lack of him.

One morning she opened the door of the little fireplace cupboard to take inventory of its state and stores. She turned over the quills and counted them; she bound the knitting-needles neatly together; she lifted the lids of the snuff canister and tobacco jar and saw that the supply for grandsir was sufficient.

Then she came upon an old pipe of Wat's— his favorite. How often she had watched him puff at it contentedly as he sat by her side. The mere sight of it, and all that it recalled oppressed her with a heavy longing for his presence. Half blinded by a sudden rush of tears, she put out her hand to the cupboard wall to steady herself, bowing her head upon her arm.

As she supported herself thus, the wall seemed to yield a little under her weight. The surprise of it aroused her. Raising her head, she scrutinized the wall intently and saw that under the

pressure that had been put upon it a single brick
had sunk back a little from its fellows, whereas
heretofore it had always been flush with them.

Her housewifely instincts awakened, she was
desirous of learning how serious a defect might
exist in the wall, and she instantly began to pry
at the brick to lift it from its place. It came out
far more easily than she had supposed could be
possible.

Peering into the cavity where the brick had
been, she was surprised to see what appeared to
be a parchment-covered object, flattened, and
firmly wedged against the inner row of bricks.
Scarcely able to credit her eyes, but with a sudden darting suspicion of what this might be that
she had so inadvertently come upon, she reached
into the cavity, closed her fingers upon the
object, and drawing it into the light, turned it
over.

A single glance confirmed her suspicions. It
was a packet, marked with the name of Dr.
Matthew Blair, and bound to it was a letter,
addressed in a wavering script to Captain
Walter Butler in the Mohawk country.

Making the guilt of Walter yet more clear, as
she turned over the packet, a tiny velvet button
dropped from between letter and packet, and

fell at her feet. Stooping to it, she instantly
recognized it as the exact match to those upon
a coat that he often wore, and which he doubtless had on upon the day when he had hidden
his booty in this place. The button must have
fallen from his sleeve at the time without his
knowledge, and slipping itself into the packet,
had remained to give evidence against him.

The excitement of her discovery drove from
her mind for the time all that had a moment
before depressed her. Here in her hand, recovered
in this most unexpected way, was the proof of
Walter's guilt, and of the truth of Watson's
dying words. Here in her hand was that which
Alison believed could never be restored to her.

She made no movement to untie the cord. That
was for Alison herself to do.

And this she should do soon, but not (and
here Mistress Butler took swift and wise
thought) until it could be done before Captain
Butler in the presence of General Johnson. Nor
would she give the packet to her, nor tell her of
it until that time. The old man should have no
room to deny his grandson's guilt, nor be able
to accuse Alison of having played some trick
upon him.

Ever so gently, and with something of reverence, Maria touched the stained and timeworn pipe upon the shelf with fingers that shook a little from the intensity of her emotion. "Ah, my Wat," she murmured, as though he were by her side, and could hear, "how are the ways of the Lord's providence wonderful and strange! Of this pipe of thine, and the pain that the sight of it has cost me, He has made tools that have opened the hiding place of the thief, and given back to the dear little one what was from her so wickedly stolen!"

Carefully she placed packet and button in the enormous outside pocket that dangled at her side. With her firm and capable hand she replaced the brick. Then she closed the cupboard door upon the place that held Walter Butler's secret for so many months, but now held it no longer.

Chapter xxiv

IT was in the morning that Mistress Butler had made her discovery. In mid-afternoon of the same day, while she and Alison, sitting on opposite sides of the hearth, were clicking their knitting-needles industriously, General Johnson, accompanied by Mark, walked in upon them.

Maria cast down her half-finished stocking, and gave both hands to her old friend. Owing to the exigencies of war, it had been months since they had met, and Mark and Alison had not seen one another since they had parted at Lake George, soon after the day of battle.

When the first warm greetings had been interchanged, Mistress Butler congratulated the General upon his new honors. "Sir William it is that I must now call thee," she observed, "but for me and thee that can make no difference."

"Will Johnson to you, Maria, always, and no frills at all between us," laughed he; and then, with a strong handclasp that spoke his sympathy, and in a deeper, lower tone, he added, "Poor

Wat! Brave as a lion he was on the day of battle. 'T is cruel hard for him and for you that he's been so sore wounded."

Mistress Butler turned away her head for an instant, to hide her brimming eyes, but recovered herself, and faced him courageously. "Ah, but he comes home!" said she simply, "and I, his wife, have pride in him."

Yet, while she listened ardently to the details that General Johnson gave her of her husband's self-sacrificing zeal on the field of battle, a zeal that had well-nigh cost him his life, and had received the joyful tidings that within the week, now, her Wat would be restored to her arms, Maria Butler did not allow herself to forget that there were wrongs of Alison's which must be redressed. Rising before long, she said, "An important matter there is, Will, that I have till thy coming kept, for thy help I must have to bring justice. Of Walter I must to his grandsir speak, and it is upon Alison's business. Wilt thou not now come?" Then turning to Alison and Mark, who had been talking in undertones of all that had happened since last they met, she added, "And thou wilt come too, my kleintje, and Mark."

General Johnson, getting to his feet with

alacrity, paused only to say, "I must be speaking
to him myself on her matters. It's in part what
I've come about."

Hearing him, Alison could not but be convinced that word had come at last from Philip
Meadowes, but there was no time for questioning. Obeying Mistress Butler, she followed them
both, with a fast-beating heart, Mark close behind her.

Captain Butler, in frowning contemplation of
the drawing-room fire, raised impatient eyebrows at this unwelcome intrusion upon his solitude, but when he saw the towering figure of
General Johnson, the asperity of his face was
tempered. Alison, reminded by the faded banian
and cap that he wore, of that dark night of her
arrival in the Mohawk, and which, but for Maria
Butler's intervention, would have had tragic
ending for her, wondered in what manner he
would receive the accusations about to be made
against his grandson.

The old soldier, prepared for lengthy converse
upon the battle, began his queries almost before
he had given the General welcome. But they were
cut short by Maria.

"Another time there will be for the battle,
grandsir," she told him, ignoring the glance of

irritation and haughty reproof that he flung her when she broke in upon him. "Now, of thy grandson, Walter, we must speak."

"Walter's matters will keep until another occasion, Maria," retorted the Captain haughtily, knitting his brows. "I wish to hear of the campaign."

"Nay," insisted Mistress Butler firmly, "it is not well that I should wait. Walter has done to Alison foul wrongs."

"We hear too much of this maid's wrongs," burst forth the Captain irascibly. He would have gone further, but Maria gave him no chance.

"Two wicked deeds lie at his door," she persisted. "Against the poor child, by his lies, he stirred up the Mohawk, Red Fox. To injure her himself, Red Fox did not dare, for William Johnson had forbade him, but he called to help him Hooting Owl, the Caughnawaga, who carried her away, perhaps, for all that Walter knew, to die."

"A pretty thing if Walter is to be held responsible for every maid that is carried off by the savages," snarled Captain Butler.

General Johnson stirred, and made as if to speak, but waited, and let Maria Butler say on.

"Besides that," she continued, "from James Watson we at last have had the truth, that it was Walter who had the little one's papers and monies stolen, and from her kept them hidden."

General Johnson half started from his chair at this, but again curbed himself to silence, and Mark, with flashing eye and curling lip, gave Alison a questioning glance. She nodded silent affirmation.

What more Maria was about to say was momentarily checked by an outburst of rage from the old man, compelled unwillingly to hear his grandchild spoken ill of.

"Stolen, woman!" he thundered from the depths of his armchair. "How dare you say such a thing of him?"

"Stolen, yes," went on Maria Butler relentlessly, "and today——"

Here she was interrupted a second time by a smooth voice from the doorway. "These be grave accusations, indeed, good aunt, if they be well-founded, but what proof can you offer of their truth?"

All looked, and saw Walter standing, booted and spurred as he had just ridden over from Fort Hunter. His supercilious glance traveled from Maria to Alison, from Alison to Mark, and back again to Maria. Then to the General and to his grandfather he yielded a respectful bow.

"For thine evil work with Red Fox we have, it is true, but the word of Hooting Owl," conceded Mistress Butler.

Walter laughed outright. "Hooting Owl! A Caughnawaga spy! Trustworthy source, indeed! Of what value, may I ask, my dear aunt, is the word of a spy?"

"Red Fox, perhaps, we can persuade to tell how true it is," suggested Maria.

"No, that you can't, Maria," interposed William Johnson. "Red Fox is dead; shot in the early morning scout. For that accusation there will be no proof."

Walter, believing the General on his side, shot him a grateful look, but General Johnson's eyes were fixed upon Maria Butler and his face betrayed nothing of his inner feeling. His words, however, had given Alison and Mark to know that they had one enemy the less.

"Of Watson, too, you spoke," continued Walter blandly, "in the same moment that you termed me thief. It may be that you prefer the word of Watson to my own."

"Not his word," interposed Alison quickly,

"his oath, as he lay dying, that he saw you with my father's monies and his papers, one morning, in your grandsir's barn."

"Oath, then," defended Walter, with a contemptuous lift of the brows. "The oath of one who played informer, for pelts, to Hooting Owl, the spy. Watson, who made his own profit on every bushel of grain or beaver-skin that he carried to my grandsir's factor. Evidence of his cheating I hold, writ in Watson's own hand. What boots the oath of such a man? Like enough if theft there were at all, Watson himself played thief, and reaped the thief's reward."

An approving smile was on the grim lips of Captain Butler as he listened to his grandson, making his defence. A clear head had young Walter, and a cool one, he thought, that made him no mean match for his accusers.

But Mistress Maria's even tones came in with disconcerting force. "The oath of Watson I have today proved true, for this I have found where thou hadst it hidden," and drawing out the packet, she held it up before the astonished gaze of all.

Alison, with a cry blent of surprise and joy, and almost incredulity, darted forward with im-

petuous, outstretched hands. Into them Mistress
Butler laid the long-lost treasure with a smile.

Astonished, and bitterly mortified at this unexpected turn in the situation, Grandsir Butler
sank back in his chair, striving to hide his dis-
comfiture.

Walter turned livid. He felt upon him the
searching scrutiny of General Johnson, for
whose good opinion he cared perhaps more than
for that of any other living creature. The hot
contempt in Mark's eyes scorched him. Maria
Butler's unflinching countenance held him ar-
raigned.

While he tried to rally his lost wits, his grandsir came to his rescue. "Whatever you have
found, Maria Wemple, as you like to call yourself," he rapped out fiercely, "the word of spies
and informers, and thieves, shall not be taken
against my boy. Of what stripe are you to try to
make out your husband's kin to be a common
rascal? And all for the sake of a dependent girl!
You shall give better proof against him than
this, or hold your peace."

At this staunch upholding of him Walter
regained something of his impudent assurance,
and prepared to brazen the matter out. "Wher-

ever you have found it, aunt," he asserted, "it was where Watson himself must have placed it."

"What I have with the packet found, against the thief gives sufficient proof," pronounced Maria Butler triumphantly. She stepped to the culprit, and lifted his right arm.

Puzzled by her act, but knowing nothing of what it might portend, Walter made no resistance.

Slipping her hand quickly into her capacious pocket, Mistress Butler drew out the tell-tale button. By a most fortuitous circumstance, the coat that he had on was the same as he had worn upon the day that he had hidden the packet. From its cuff a button was missing. Mistress Butler fitted to the empty place the button she had found. It matched the others to perfection.

With the eyes of all upon him, Walter, fairly trapped as he was, would still vehemently have protested his innocence, but Captain Butler brusquely cut him short.

"Say no more of it, Walter," he commanded. "You're caught. Admit it."

"But hear you," he went on, addressing the rest haughtily, "the boy's no thief. He's done this, as anyone can see, merely to pay off old scores. The maid flouted him, most like, when

he meant to be civil. To pay her off, he hid her
packet, till he should see fit to restore it. Call it
revenge, if you will, and a boy's lie to cover it,
but no worse. As to the matter of Red Fox and
Hooting Owl there 's naught proved against him,
so let's hear no more on that."

With the air of one who has closed a disagreeable piece of business to his complete satisfaction, and vindicated one who had been un-
justly taken to task, the old man extended claw-
like fingers to Alison. "You hold a letter and
papers sent me by your father, girl. Let's have
them."

Loth to obey him, yet remembering her
father's charge, Alison went to him, and gave
them over to his imperious hand.

Mistress Maria had not yet done, however.
She fixed her blue eyes, by nature warm and
kind, but now as cold as ice, upon Walter, where
he stood accepting the excuses that his grandfather made for him, and wearing the air of one
whose very small peccadillo has been magnified
by his ill-wishers into a criminal act.

"Outrageous meanness it was," she contested,
"and that we all know, whatever by it was intended. A sweet young maid he has shamefully
treated, and you, grandsir, would have him to go

unpunished. But I, Maria Wemple, say this: at least he shall come no more under this roof while Alison it covers."

Captain Butler, about to forbid peremptorily any such banishment, bethought himself in time. He was old and self-indulgent. Upon Maria, excellent housekeeper, and nurse, depended all the care of the household, and all provision for his creature comforts. Alison need not remain long enough now to greatly interfere with his grandson's comings and goings. So he checked the outward expression of his resentment, and let Maria's ruling stand.

Walter favored Mistress Butler with a sweeping bow. " 'T is a soft punishment that you inflict upon me, aunt, for my very great crime," he said ironically. With that, he turned upon his heel and was gone.

Amid the silence of the rest, Captain Butler turned his attention to the contents of the packet, with a great rattling of its parchment cover, and slow examination of the monies and papers. With the deliberation of the aged he read through Matthew Blair's letter, but with no softening of his iron countenance. When at length he had finished his inspection, he wrapped the whole together, and was about to place the packet in his banian.

At this William Johnson leaned forward.

"One moment, Captain," he said suavely. "I have lately received a letter concerning these properties of Alison's which will interest you, and will, moreover, relieve you of all care and responsibility concerning them."

The old man threw back his head sharply and raised his shaggy eyebrows. "Indeed!" he ejaculated, "and what may that be?" Now that he had learned the value of the packet's contents, he was by no means anxious to have the disposal of these monies taken out of his control.

"Some little while ago," began Johnson, laying his hand affectionately upon Alison's, "this lass confided to me that she had received no answer to her many letters writ to Dr. Philip Meadowes, in England. To comfort her, and relieve you, sir, of a trouble, I, myself, sent him an urgent letter by a trustworthy messenger. He has writ me saying that no letter from her had ever been received by him. He gives my letter to Mr. Morrison, solicitor to Dr. Blair, and this gentleman has writ me that by the terms of her father's will, he is become her guardian. She being absent from England, he makes me for the time being his proxy, to care for her and whatever properties she has this side the water, and to get her back to England as soon as there's good voyaging."

"I see that these come to you, then," admitted Captain Butler, as with ill-concealed chagrin he surrendered the packet. "You need not have put yourself to such trouble, Will. I could have managed it."

"No trouble, sir," the General assured him courteously, slipping the packet into a safe place within his broadcloth coat.

Mistress Butler gave a long-drawn sigh of relief. It was true that Walter was to escape his just deserts, but at any rate Alison's properties were now in safe hands, and she would come again into the happy security that was her right.

As for Alison, joy, almost too great to be borne, swept over her in a flood. Once more she was free to be her bright young self: free to go home to Kent! To the dear old garden, to Roger, to Martha, to all her old, well-loved friends! Here she paused: her father, who had given meaning to every detail of her life at home, was not to be there now; was gone, never to return.

A sharp pang shot through her heart. Yet in a moment the consoling truth came to her, that still his love would flow out to her, still she could follow his noble teachings, and that in that very real sense he would always be with her wherever she might go.

Pain there would be in leaving dear Mistress Butler, and it would be hard to bid good-bye to Nan and Mary, to the General, and, above all, Mark; Mark—who sat looking at his cuff, plunged in deep thought. Hard, indeed it would be, to say farewell to him.

She was thinking of it still, when, a moment later, having left Grandsir Butler to himself, they stood in a little group by the kitchen hearth. As if reading her thoughts, General Johnson suddenly turned to her, and queried, with a smile, "What would you be saying, dear lass, if this lad, here, should be making the voyage with you, when you go home to England?" As he spoke he laid his broad hand upon Mark's sturdy shoulder.

"With me? To England?" exclaimed Alison, wide-eyed.

"To England!" echoed Mark, no less amazed than she.

"Yes, to England. And for this, lad," said Sir

William, with emphasis, "you've gifts beyond clerk's business. Surgeon Williams had an eye on your good work among the wounded up at camp there. 'T was his opinion, given to me, that a rare good doctor and chirurgeon would be lost in an excellent clerk. So I'm packing you off in the Spring with Alison, to read with Dr. Philip Meadowes, since we've no proper schooling for such work, as yet, this side the water. And there you're to stay, if you're so minded, till you've finished your studies, and walked at St. Bart's for your experience."

Dumbfounded at this unparalleled good fortune, Mark had no wits left either to give thanks or to answer. Speechless with gratitude, he could only stand and stare at his benefactor.

"And when you've got your sheepskin," went on the General, "you'll come back again, and look after us here, for we've sore need of good doctors."

"Oh, Mark!" rejoiced Alison.

"Oh, General Johnson!" stammered Mark, finding voice at last. " 'T is a marvelous kindness that you do me!"

"Nay, lad. 'T is but your just desert for good and brave service in time of battle," replied Sir William. "Take it so."

After they two had departed, Alison went to where Maria Butler had sunk down upon the settle, and knelt beside her.

"Wouldst have me stay with thee, till Spring, dear Mistress Butler?" she asked, her arch face lifted.

"Ah, that thou must," replied Maria tenderly. " 'T will not be safe voyaging till then.

"Go thou must, to thine own land, my kleintje, that I know," she went on soberly, stroking the velvet cheek close to her own. "But wilt thou not come back, perhaps, some day, to see the friends who love thee, here?"

"Happen I may," smiled Alison, stealing comforting arms about her. "Happen I may."